THE DECEIVED WIFE

Sharon L. Snyder

ISBN: 1979144591
ISBN 13: 9781979144599

Based on a true story with some fiction added. All names have been changed to protect identities.

CHAPTER ONE

June, 1964

I was sitting in my bedroom applying oil paint to a clear jar, listening to the Elvis Presley song 'She's Not You' and daydreaming about the boy I had a crush on at our school when suddenly I heard a door slam and my father's voice boomed, echoing throughout the house. "What do you mean; you don't know where she is?"

Startled, I accidentally dropped my hand, smearing the red paint and ruining the rose I was attempting to draw on the jar. I fumbled with the cloth, trying to clean the mess before I stood up and hurried to the door. Pulling it open slightly, I stuck my head out and listened. I could barely hear my mother's voice. It sounded like she was crying and I was curious to know why.

Easing the door all the way open, I stepped out into the hallway. As I approached the living room, I heard my mother say, "Honestly, Bashir, I thought she was spending the week with Farhana. How was I to know she wasn't there? She's always been responsible to go directly to her house and stay there." I could hear mother sighing deeply between sobs. Farhana was our aunt by marriage; my father's older brother's wife.

"Well, Saida, she isn't there now and I want to know the whereabouts of my precious daughter, Salima. If something has happened to her, I'll never get over it." Father's voice became more reflective. He was running his hand over his face as I peeked around the corner.

I knew my father was totally distressed by the disappearance of his favorite child, Salima, who also happened to be the oldest. It seemed his love for her was way beyond what he felt for his other children; me and my three brothers. Father seemed intolerant of me or perhaps it was that he didn't acknowledge my presence, and therefore I perceived that he didn't love me at all. My self-esteem was at an all-time low at that point in my life.

My father, Bashir Jan, was an important figure in our town of Rawalpindi, Pakistan. Well respected in the community, he was a chief judge who was also feared by those who broke the law. At fourteen years of age, my fear of him was just as strong as if I'd been a criminal, too.

Our country was very modern at the time, long before the Taliban took control of things there. We dressed in Western style clothing and boys and girls attended school together. In fact, although our family was Muslim, our school was a Catholic run facility. It was a private convent school and we were taught by the nuns.

I liked the fact that we had to wear uniforms, because they were blue shirts over white shalwars. The shalwar is loose, pajama-like trousers. We wore a v-shaped white scarf called a dopata over the shirt.

I had become infatuated with the boy who sat beside me in the class. His name was Farook and he had the most piercing black eyes I'd ever seen. I could tell he liked me, too. The looks he gave me indicated he was very interested. One day, he came up to me while we were leaving the school and held my hand. My heart had swooned and I felt light headed. I thought it must be love. I had begun thinking about him every day whenever I wasn't concentrating on my schoolwork. I daydreamed that when I got older, I'd be married to him. If something bad happened to Salima and caused my dreams to be shattered, I'd never forgive her.

I walked into the living room where my parents were sitting. "Ammi, are you alright? I thought I heard you crying." I sat down close to my mom and held her hand.

My father turned and with a cursory glance at me, he nodded his head to indicate I should leave the room. He had a scowl on his face when he turned his attention back to my ammi; my mother. "Your ammi and I are having a private conversation," he said, barely looking at me.

I lowered my head, but kept my eyes on ammi's face. She put her arm around me and pulled me to her side. "Let her stay. She needs to know about her sister's disappearance."

Tears sprang into my eyes. As much as I disliked my sister, I didn't want her to die. "Abba, I'm sorry," I said as I leaned in closer to my ammi's side. "Should we all go look for her?"

"I wouldn't know where to begin looking," he said as he took a seat on the beige and golden tone sofa and crossed his knees. The look of stress on his face was disturbing to me. My abba had always been a power house of resolute constitution. At that moment, I felt tenderness toward the father I so feared. Not that he was mean or abusive to me, but on the rare occasions when he did acknowledge me, he would always put me down; telling me I'm not as pretty or as smart as my sister, Salima.

The front door opened and my younger brothers all bounded into the room. Zahid, Ali and Adnan scuttled across the floor toward my father. Typical boys, they were dirty and sweaty from playing soccer in the field at the end of the street. I would normally have been out with them, but I had not been feeling well that morning, so I'd stayed inside and painted instead.

Waving them away from the furniture, he said, "Go get cleaned up before dinner. Abbiee has already prepared your clothes for the evening." Abbiee was our governess and she always made sure we looked our best when we were not outside playing. Just then, as though on cue, Abbiee stepped into view and motioned the boys toward their rooms.

"Hurry up, boys. I've laid out your clothes already." Abbiee was waiting for them to follow her.

"Yes, Ma'am," the three boys said in unison as they scampered toward her.

Our house was large with six bedrooms, so everyone got their own room, except the two youngest boys. One bedroom was shared by our governess, Abbiee and our cook, Zareen. Since we were a wealthy family, my ammi spent a lot of her time doing charity work which was expected of an affluent woman in those days.

Shoving and trying to trip each other, my brothers followed Abbiee out of the room to clean up for dinner. As soon as they left, Abba gave me a stern look and said, "You need to prepare yourself for dinner, also. Your ammi and I have a few things to finish discussing in private."

I stood up and gave Ammi a sympathetic look before I sauntered back to my room. Deep in conflicting thoughts, I began putting my oil paints away. I couldn't help but think of my spoiled sister who got away with anything and everything. And she was quite capable of doing almost anything she pleased.

I dressed in my prettiest green shalwar kamiz. Although the sari is commonly worn by women, the shalwar kamiz, which is a combination of calf-length shirt and baggy silk pants, are favored by girls and young women. Afterward, I sat staring at my reflection, in the mirror. I had been told I was pretty, but I just couldn't see it. Although, as I scrutinized my features, I thought my dark brown, almond shaped eyes did look lovely, especially when I wore makeup. Running a brush through my thick, dark brown hair, I felt fortunate to have it as my crowning glory.

I heard my Ringneck parrot saying something, so I got up and went to his cage. I had placed it near the window, so he could get a lot of light and see outside. I stuck my index finger in the cage and stroked his green feathers. Spending time with my parrot gave me a calm feeling. When I was distressed I would talk to him and tell some of my secret thoughts. He talked to me, but never divulged any of my secrets, especially when Abbiee was in my room.

My brothers were running through the hallway, so I figured dinner must be ready. I opened my door and could smell the delicious food Zareen had prepared for us. I walked slowly toward the dining room in hopes that my ammi was feeling calmer now.

Our dining table was laden with a feast; curried chicken and daal dominated the center of the table with salad and fruits of various types; melons, pears and apples. A platter of naan, which is a type of bread, was placed beside the chicken. I especially loved the daal which was made from lentils. A bowl of chutney was placed next to the chicken. It was a type of relish made from different vegetables and was usually very spicy.

I took my place at the table and heaped a mound of daal on my plate along with a chicken breast and some naan. Then I scooped some salad out and took some of the fruit. I was very pleased to see that Zareen had made rice pudding for dessert. Thoughts of Salima ceased as I dug into the food and savored the taste.

Ammi was very quiet during dinner and no one seemed brave enough to talk to her, although every now and then Abba would say something to her; mostly something trivial.

When dinner was over, I excused myself and went to my room. I'd learned nothing new about my sister's whereabouts. I began to have different visions of her antics and each one put her at grave risk. Finally, I decided that whatever she had done, she deserved the consequences. As I took off the shalwar kamiz and slipped into my pajamas I smiled at the thought of seeing my friend in the morning. Farook was very handsome in my opinion and I'd grown fond of staring at him without anyone noticing.

I sat down at my desk and wrote in my diary. I let the anguish and hurt feelings I normally felt flow onto the pages as I released my angst about my life in general, and Salima in particular. My eyelids grew heavy, so I shut the diary and put it away.

Walking to my bed, I pulled the covers back and slid into it. I immediately closed my eyes and conjured up Farook's face. I fell asleep almost immediately, but my dreams weren't about him. They were nightmarish about Salima and the predicament she was in. Each time I awoke and went back to sleep, there was a new development in her dilemma.

When morning dawned, I opened my eyes and was so disgusted with the dreams I'd encountered all night that I secretly wished Salima would never come home. I felt a twinge of regret at thinking such a thing as I threw back the covers and stepped into my slippers at the bedside.

As soon as I dressed, I headed straight for the kitchen and ate breakfast. Abbiee was sitting there with Zareen and I asked her if she'd overheard anything about Salima. "No, I haven't heard a thing," Abbiee said as she picked up her teacup and took a sip. Her gray hair was pulled back into a bun at the back of her head. Her brown eyes gleamed when she smiled at me. "Don't worry, little one. I'm sure your sister is alright. You know how she likes to create havoc. It's a good thing her fiancé's parents are in Karachi and not here in Rawalpindi."

A common practice in Pakistan, Salima was engaged to be married to our first cousin, Rashid Ahmed. He was older by several years and had already graduated from medical school. He had left to further his education in the United States.

"Yes, I guess that's for the best. If they knew of her dalliances, they might not want her as a daughter-in-law." I laughed softly. "Of course, they can't do anything about the fact that she's their niece." I took the last bite of my breakfast and went to brush my teeth and get ready for the last day of the school year.

Although my father was quite liberal, he and my mother prayed five times a day, as is the custom in Muslim culture. However, Abba was not strict about his children praying that many times a day. I didn't feel very religious and only enjoyed some of the holiday feasts.

Abba and Ammi were on their mats praying as I hurried out of the house ahead of my brothers and dashed to the waiting car, giving a cursory glance at the policeman who guarded our gate. Our chauffeur held the car door open for us to climb in and as soon as we were seated, he drove us to school. I wanted our driver to go a little faster so I could spend some extra time around Farook, if possible, since I wouldn't see much of him until the next school session started.

My heart did a flip when I saw him standing close to the school building looking in my direction. I bounded out of the car as soon as our driver opened the door and headed straight for him, but was intercepted by my younger brother, Zahid, who grabbed my arm, holding me back.

I looked into his dark eyes and said, "What do you want? I don't want to be late."

"Ambreen, just before we left, I overheard Ammi telling Abbiee that Salima came home very early this morning and went straight to bed," he whispered. Zahid was the oldest of my three brothers. He was already slightly taller than me.

"Well, good for her!" I stammered, staring Zahid in the eyes. "I'm sure she'll have quite a story to convey now that she's back. I wish she would have just stayed wherever she has been." I folded my arms and stood ramrod straight.

"Don't be so mean about her. She is our sister," Zahid said, a small smile curling the edges of his mouth.

"I know, but she's so infuriating sometimes and gets away with anything she wants." When I turned to look back at Farook, he was gone. Now my day was truly ruined. Salima returning and Farook disappearing was not what I had wished for that day.

My Abba's job was a government job and so we were moved from one city to another every five or six years, it seemed. I'd been born in Peshawar close to the Afghanistan border and had lived there until about the age of five. Now we were living in Rawalpindi which is situated at the foothills of the Himalayas. The summers were long and very hot with monsoon rains. Thunderstorms almost seemed like a daily occurrence.

Since it was summer, the temperature in Rawalpindi was already 82 degrees and it was still morning. I needed to get inside and cool down.

I made a mad dash for the front door and hurried to my classroom. Farook was already sitting at his desk. His book was open in front of him. When I walked to my seat, he didn't even look up at me. I felt crushed that his interest in me was only fleeting. I made up my mind that I would use a conscious effort to rid him from my mind over the summer.

When school ended that day, I picked up my books and scampered into the car that awaited us. Our driver seemed to be in a hurry and we made it home in record time. Before going in the house, I stopped in our garden and sat on a bench under the evergreen Ashoka tree to contemplate how I felt about Farook. The sweet smell of the tree's yellow tube-like lobed flowers assaulted my nose, and I inhaled deeply.

The fragrance gave me a little boost in my mood, and I made the decision that I would find someone else to think about as a future husband. I stood up, plucked a purple Lajwanti flower from its stem and carried it into the house. Placing it in a vase of water, I carried it to my bedroom and put it on my window sill.

CHAPTER TWO

Salima was sitting in the living room as I was walking through to the kitchen. I was hungry and wanted one of Zareen's after school snacks. I wanted to avoid looking at her, but she spoke and I reflexively glanced at her. "Ambreen, aren't you going to speak to me?"

"I hadn't planned to." I sneered at her and kept walking.

"Don't you want to hear my good news?" Salima said, inclining back on the sofa and crossing her arms. She tilted her head to the side as a huge smile filled the bottom of her face. Her dark brown hair was pulled back off her forehead and her dark brown eyes had a gleam in them.

Curious about where she'd been and what she'd been up to, I plopped down on a chair and said, "Sure. Tell me all the details of your misadventure, Salima." I leaned back and crossed my ankles. I was sure this was going to be some story and I didn't want to miss a word.

"I'm going to marry Mahmood," Salima said, putting emphasis on his name. She had a smug look on her face.

"What?" I became momentarily speechless. When I recovered, I said, "Mahmood? You mean Chachi Farhana's brother? How is that possible? You're engaged to Rashid. The family will never stand for this."

"I've already spoken to Abba and Ammi about it. Abba was angry with me at first, but I told him I'd take a bottle of pills and end my life if he didn't let me marry Mahmood. Abba wasn't happy about that, but I finally convinced him to let me marry the man I love. They relented and said it would be fine and that I could marry Mahmood if I wanted. Besides he's the love of my life."

"So, is that where you've been recently? With him?" I gave her a look of disdain. I marveled at how she could convince Abba to agree to anything she wanted, when he didn't even acknowledge my existence most of the time.

"Yes, but not like you think. He took me to a special place and we slept in separate quarters." Her smug smile irritated me and I wanted to wipe it off her face.

"So, what are you going to do about our cousin, Rashid? Chacha Laeeq and Chachi Sheeba will not be pleased. How will you smooth things over with them?" My mind was a bee hive of activity. I was imagining various scenarios and each one had a terrible consequence. Chacha Laeeq was known to be a very stern and religious man who spent much time in the mosque after he got off work. I could not imagine he would take the news well.

Chachi Sheeba was my abba's sister and she may cause a rift with our families as well, if she was unpleased by this turn of events. Oh well, I thought, it's not my problem.

"I'm sure it will be fine. I never hear from Rashid anyway, so he probably won't care. You know he's in the United States now anyway. He's furthering his education there." She paused and looked me in the eyes. "Chacha and Chachi will just have to accept that this is the way it's going to be. I'm sure they'll find another wife for him in the near future."

I didn't know our cousin Rashid very well. I'd only seen him on a few occasions and, since he was ten years older than me, we'd never had any interaction when we were in the same house. His two sisters and three brothers were closer to my age, and I knew them a little better at the time. I did feel sorry for Rashid, however. I had visions of him feeling dejected and pining away for Salima. At least he was away in the United States, and although he would probably be shocked to hear the news, he would most likely be so busy that he would recover quickly.

"So, when are you planning to marry Mahmood?" I asked as I twirled a lock of hair around my right index finger. "What does Chachi Farhana think about this; you marrying her brother?"

"We are planning to marry next year and Chachi Farhana is excited about it. She's known for quite some time that we've had feelings for each other. She's pleased Mahmood has found happiness now." Salima stood up and started walking toward her room. "We'll talk some more later, sis."

Salima was shorter than me, and heavier. I wouldn't say she was fat, but she was definitely somewhat chunky. Thankful that I was slender, I watched her swaying down the hallway before I got up and went into the kitchen. I snatched a cookie off the platter Zareen had sitting on the counter. I bit into it and promptly spit it out in the trash, tossing the rest of it out, too. I had lost my appetite after my conversation with Salima. It just amazed me how she could control people and always get her way. It was astonishing how she could affect so many lives and never give it a second thought.

Ammi was just coming in the front door as I emerged from the kitchen. She looked tired and sad. She sat down in one of the chairs in the living room after slipping off her shoes. Rubbing them together, she said, "I've had a tiring day. Would you ask Zareen to make me a cup of tea?"

"Of course, Ammi," I said as I poked my head through the kitchen door and called to Zareen. As soon as I told her Ammi wanted tea, I returned and sat on a chair close to my ammi. "Were you busy with your charity work today," I asked as I reached for her hand.

"Yes, it was exhausting dealing with all the poor people who needed help. As soon as I drink my tea, I'm going to rest and maybe take a nap before dinner."

"Salima told me she's going to marry Mahmood. Are you and Abba really okay with her breaking her engagement to Rashid and going through with this marriage to Chachi Farhana's brother?" I knew I was pushing it to ask such questions of my ammi, but I'd always felt close to her and knew she'd likely be honest with me.

"Your abba and I were surprised to learn that she's in love with Mahmood and wants to marry him. At first, Bashir was extremely angry with Salima, but she cried and said she'd take a bottle of sleeping pills if she couldn't marry Mahmood, so he relented and gave her permission. If she'll be happier with him than with Rashid, then we should let her be with the man who will make her a happy wife."

Zareen brought in the tea and poured a cup for my ammi. She offered me a cup and I accepted. As we sat there sipping our tea, Ammi starting telling me about the plans for Salima's wedding that they had discussed earlier in the day. It would take place sometime close the beginning of next year.

I excused myself and went to my room. Shutting the door, I threw myself across the bed and cried. Somehow, I felt that Salima getting her way with this marriage was not going to go well for me. I didn't know how that would be, but a sinking feeling settled over me, and I felt like screaming.

Finally, bringing myself out of the snit I was in, I thought I was being silly to entertain such beliefs. How could Salima's engagement and marriage to Mahmood affect me in any way?

In the bathroom, I washed my face so no one could tell I'd been crying. I talked to my parrot, Mittu, and told him of my fears. He was such a patient bird; staying perched on my shoulder while I expressed my feelings to him. After divulging my deepest feelings, I felt foolish and began to feel my spirits lift. I was determined to be in a good mood the rest of the evening.

Abbiee knocked softly at my door and pried it open slightly. "Ambreen, are you ready for dinner? I was getting concerned about you, since you've been sequestered in your room after coming home from school."

"I'm coming, Abbiee. I just finished getting dressed for dinner." I walked out into the hallway with Abbiee and into the dining room where my abba and Salima were already sitting at the table.

"I'm so happy to have you back home," Abba said, looking directly at Salima. "You are such a beautiful girl with red cheeks like apples. I'm sure the whole world would appreciate your beauty." He was smiling like a Cheshire cat, the fictional cat known for its distinctive mischievous grin.

I instinctively covered my nose with the palm of my left hand as I took my seat at the table. I was very sensitive about my nose which seemed a little too long to me. Abba never commented about my looks, so I assumed I wasn't worthy of praise like my sister. I was always worrying about how I looked at that time.

My mind flashed back to the time in fifth grade when I'd been selected to play Grandma in the play 'Little Red Riding Hood' because of my long nose. There had been many times in my life that I'd put a handkerchief over my nose to hide it. I felt like slipping down under the table, but I feared Abba would disapprove, if I did something foolish.

"So, Salima," my abba said, "what caused you to be attracted to Farhana's brother, Mahmood? Was it his army uniform? It seems young girls go crazy over a man in uniform now days." He picked up the ladle and spooned rice onto his plate.

"Well, yes, Abba, that's the first thing that attracted me to him, but he's so caring and kind that he won my heart. He's so much younger than Chachi Farhana, too."

I thought Mahmood was a very nice, young man, also, and thought maybe having him for a brother-in-law would be a nice thing. I even entertained the idea that my life would improve with Salima out of the house. Deep in thought, I jumped slightly when I heard my abba's voice.

"I'm hosting a party tomorrow night. The famous classical singer, Malika will be here along with the television star, Feroza. I want all of you children to be on your best behavior." Abba speared a piece of chapli kebab which had been made from ground beef.

"Oh, I love the way Malika sings," Ammi said as she took her place at the table and put her napkin on her lap.

Zahid, Ali and Adnan all had an excited look on their faces. We all loved Abba's parties because we got to dance and enjoy our friends company. "May we invite our friends again?" Zahid asked as he tore off a piece of Naan and brought it toward his mouth.

"Of course," Abba replied. "Invite all your friends, boys and girls. We'll dance the night away doing the twist and the cha-cha." Abba was quite modern in his thinking and loved dancing and being entertained. Having a good time was of upmost importance to him, it seemed.

"Laila, our cousin from the USA is coming tomorrow, too. I'm excited to see her. It's been so long since we met with her." Ammi picked up the fruit platter and transferred some pieces of pears and apples to her plate.

I smiled at the thought of seeing Laila. She was such an impressive person as well as being highly educated with a PhD. We all looked up to her and felt that whatever she said, it was coming from God.

When dinner was finished, I hurried back to my room. I had to plan for the party the next night. Rummaging through my closet, I selected the outfit I would wear. Then I called my friends and invited them to the party. I was enthralled with excitement.

"Abba is having a party tomorrow night and I'd like you and your brother to attend," I said when my close friend, Rue answered the phone. "Please say you'll come. It'll be such fun."

"I can probably go," Rue said. "I'll ask my parents, but I'm sure they'll let us. See you tomorrow night."

The next night, Abba's bash went off with great enthusiasm by all who attended. We ate so much delicious Pakistani food and danced until we nearly dropped. Malika sang such beautiful songs and Feroza kept us entertained as well.

"Are you enjoying the party, Ambreen?" Ammi asked as she walked over toward the table. "I see you've been dancing the whole evening."

"Yes, Ammi, I am enjoying it," I replied with a huge smile on my face. I was going to say something else to her, but our cousin, Laila came over and said, "Saida, this is one of the best parties I've been to in a long time. I'm so glad I could come."

"You should come home to Pakistan more often, Laila," Ammi said and then she excused herself to go check on some other guests who arrived late.

It was such an exciting evening, but the main highlight of the night for me was when our cousin Laila turned to me and said, "You are so beautiful, Ambreen. You're more beautiful than your sister. You have very classic features."

"Thank you," I muttered, hardly believing my ears. Was it true someone thought I was beautiful? I felt like I was walking on clouds the rest of the evening. I fell into bed later that night feeling exhausted, but blissfully happy for the first time in as long as I could remember.

When I awoke the next morning, I popped up out of bed and dressed in my old clothes for riding bikes. My brothers and I were planning to race against some of the neighborhood kids. It was exhilarating to fly over the terrain, the wind blowing on my face. At that moment, I couldn't have been any happier.

CHAPTER THREE

The summer whizzed past and soon it was time for school to begin again. The school year began in September and ended in June. I loved the beginning of the school year, because my birthday was in September. I'd be turning 15 very soon and looked forward to the day I'd be an adult and could get married. All of us girls had the idea that marriage was fun. You got to wear nice clothes and enjoy life. Not being grounded in reality, none of us ever thought anything bad could happen in a marriage.

The first day of school, I saw Farook and noticed he was watching another girl in our class. I was glad I'd gotten over him during the long, hot summer months. I'd begun to have a crush on a neighbor boy who played with my brothers and me.

On my birthday, I was surprised with a gift of jewelry; necklace and earrings. It looked very costly and glittered when I held it to the light. It was definitely gold with small sapphires set in them. The rich blue color of my birthstone looked wonderful next to my dark brown hair. Once, I'd read that during the Middle Ages the gem Sapphire was believed to protect those close to you and keep them from harm, but also represented loyalty and trust. I thought of myself as fiercely loyal as I put them on and admired myself in the mirror. It was my most treasured gift, although I'd also received clothing and makeup.

"Thank you, Abba and Ammi, for the wonderful birthday gifts," I said as I displayed my new jewelry for everyone to see.

"You're welcome," Ammi said as she picked up a slice of cake from the buffet table. Abba just glanced at me and said nothing.

That fall, my parents were busy with wedding plans for Salima's upcoming marriage. Invitations were sent out and caterers were engaged for the event. I kept myself busy with school work and the activities I had signed up for. I tried not to think about Salima's wedding plans. The less I knew about them, the better, I thought. If I admitted it, I guess I was a little jealous that she could get her way and choose who she would marry. Then guilt would attack my conscience and I'd feel sorry for my thoughts.

The school year started to go by in a blur until Ramadan began in January of 1965. The ninth month of the Islamic lunar calendar, Ramadan is the month of fasting to commemorate the first revelations of the Quran to Muhammad. When the crescent moon, or new moon, is seen at sunset, then the month begins. Everyone is obligated to fast for the entire month from sunrise to sunset, except for those who are ill, elderly, diabetic, or pregnant. Children up to a certain age were also exempt.

I was old enough to have to observe the ritual, so we were made to arise from bed early in order to eat a big breakfast. The days were shorter in January, so I was thankful we didn't have to fast for so many hours. No food or drink was allowed during the daylight and it could be very difficult to refrain from wanting even a glass of water.

Every day that month, I adhered to the rules and ate only before sunrise and after sunset. There was always a large amount of food on the table for our dinner as soon as the sun went down. I ate greedily at times and earned a scornful look from my abba. Not wanting to disappoint him or make him more critical of me, I learned to eat smaller amounts and appear to be a dainty eater. Soon, I learned to eat only small portions all the time.

Finally, February arrived and soon thereafter the month of Ramadan ended. For the next three days, there was a feast to celebrate. The festival of breaking the fast is called Eid al-Fitr and it starts the first day of the next month, Shawwal. It is considered the most important religious holiday in Islam.

There is a particular Islamic prayer that may be performed only in a congregation. However, prior to the prayers, Muslims are obligated to offer zakat which is an offering for the poor and needy. Giving to charity helps to provide emergency food, shelter and other amenities for others such as refugees. I was mindful of the tenet and procured some of my own money to donate to charity. I tried to feel appreciative of the blessings Allah had bestowed on me.

I never felt particularly religious, but I adhered to all the tenets of Islam just in case it was all true. I wouldn't want to be banned from heaven for not believing or doing what was expected of me.

I was so excited to begin the three-day festival of Eid al-Fatr in which I had shopped for new clothes and bought perfume to wear. I bought gifts for relatives and lavished some on our servants. I was sure Allah would be pleased with me.

Abba had bought an expensive perfume for the festival and he proudly brought it into the living room where I was sitting with my ammi and Salima. "I bought this delightful smelling perfume for us. Wait until you smell it," Abba said as he took the cap off and walked toward Salima and sprayed it.

"Oh, that's wonderful, Abba," Salima said, smiling as she inhaled deeply.

Then he walked to Ammi and sprayed some on her. "I love how it smells, Bashir," she said, tilting her head down in order to get a better whiff of it.

I expected Abba to spray some perfume on me next; however, I was shocked when he sprayed himself and then put the bottle away. He truly doesn't even know I exist, I thought with bitterness.

"Let's hurry and indulge in the feast tonight," he said and then left the room. Used to feeling excluded, I brushed the hurt feelings aside and concentrated on the festival.

Our feasts consisted of wonderful Pakistani dishes including many sweets. We indulged in so much food, I felt like I had to waddle home to my room after the holiday was over. I had thoroughly enjoyed celebrating with so many of our friends and relatives during the holiday; therefore, I felt that nothing could hamper my happiness at the moment.

Almost before I knew it, the wedding date was fast arriving and I would be gaining a brother-in-law. I was pleased that Salima would have a husband to concentrate on and not pick on me.

Shortly before the wedding, a bridal henna party was given. A joyful occasion, intricate designs or patterns are applied to the hands of the bride and bridesmaids, with the bride receiving the most intricate patterns.

Believed that henna gives blessings, luck and joy, it is also seen as a beauty enhancer. As the henna paste dries and flakes off, it leaves the skin stained with the designs which the artist has created.

Salima had to sit perfectly still for a long period of time, so her friends danced and sang songs to entertain her. Several times, one of her friends brought a treat for her and popped it into her mouth. Each time, Salima smiled and thanked them. I smiled as I thought of possibly throwing a tart in her face so I could watch her jump and smear the henna. I immediately felt remorseful and wished I'd not thought that.

When her hands were finished having henna designs placed on them, I walked over and looked to see if the artist had tattooed Mahmood's name on her. Sure enough, his name was integrated into the patterns.

The day before the wedding, Salima stuck her head into my room and said, "So, little sis, aren't you just so jealous of me now. I get to marry the person I want. I don't have to be stuck marrying an old cousin. If you try, maybe you can convince Abba to let you marry whoever you want when you're old enough." She giggled and put her hands on her hips. "But don't count on it, sis." I knew she was just being spiteful and chose to ignore what she said.

"No, Salima, I'm not jealous of you," I said. I really wanted to say more, but I decided it wasn't worth fighting with her.

That night we both remained civil to one another. I supposed she was nervous, and I was not in the mood for her bantering. We went to bed that night with excitement in our hearts; Salima at getting married and me thinking I'd be getting rid of Salima.

Mahmood and Salima's wedding was a big event. There were more than one hundred people in attendance. Although most Pakistani brides choose to wear red dresses for their weddings, Salima chose green. I must say, it was beautiful with silver thread embroidered throughout the dress.

Heavy gold jewelry was draped around her neck and hung from her ears. Her head was covered with a thin material matching her dress. When I saw her coming into the large tent that was set up on our property, I was awe struck. Salima looked more beautiful than I'd ever seen her. I glanced at Abba and could see he was bursting with pride.

I walked to the side of the tent and peeked out when I heard the drums rhythmic cadence. Mahmood and his family were arriving at the wedding and were greeted with rose petals. I was happy to see that Mahmood had dressed in a Western style suit.

The Imam, a Muslim priest, had the bride and groom sign the marriage contract during the ceremony. Afterwards, dinner was served which consisted of several meat dishes including chicken, lamb and various forms of kebabs.

Music and dancing went on for hours until finally Salima and Mahmood left for his parent's house. I went to bed that night dreaming of the day I would have my own wedding ceremony. It couldn't happen any too soon in my opinion.

A couple of days later, Mahmood and Salima hosted a dinner to celebrate their consummation as husband and wife. Mahmood's parents helped him organize the event and invited all of our family and guests to their home for the feast. This is done typically to publicize the marriage.

When we arrived, Salima was dressed in a heavily decorated dress with gold jewelry which had been provided by Mahmood's family. The groom was dressed in a tuxedo. They were then publicly show-cased as a married couple.

Mahmood and Salima then left for a short honeymoon. When they returned, Salima came and announced she was moving her things out of our house. Mahmood was being stationed elsewhere in the country and she was happy for the new adventure in her life. I sat idly by and watched as she and her new husband carried all her belongings out of our house. Good riddance, I thought to myself. Now she wouldn't be there to put me down all the time.

While my sister was gathering some of her clothing, Mahmood came and sat close to me in the living room. "My little sister is looking so beautiful today. All made up and hair styled. Wow," he said, smiling.

My heart swooned at such a wonderful compliment and to think it was my own sister's husband who had said such kind words. I could hardly believe it for a moment. When I regained my wits about me, I thanked him modestly and smiled. After having both Laila and Mahmood affirm that I was pretty, I began to have more confidence in myself and stopped thinking I was ugly. Never again would I think I was less than others.

Salima came into the room and offered me a weak smile. "Maybe someday soon you'll find some happiness, too, Ambreen," she said, sitting down beside Mahmood and looking straight at me. "Of course, I don't suspect you'll find as wonderful a husband as I've found now."

"I'll find my own happiness, Salima," I said as I glared back at her. "At least I won't have to marry any man you select for me." I had an urge to stick my tongue out at her, but common sense forbade me to do that. Someday I would have my revenge, I thought.

A short time after Salima moved out, Abba came home one day and announced we would be moving to Mardan soon. The courts needed to transfer him in the near future. I was devastated. I would have to leave my friends and the boy I had a crush on at that moment.

The movers came and packed up all our belongings; stowing them in a large moving truck. Finally, we were on our way to a new home and hopefully, new friends.

I began to have a sense of adventure as the car we were riding in went around hills and through towns. Maybe I would really love the place after all.

I was disappointed when we arrived in Mardan and saw that it was a small town. But the house we were going to be living in was very large, and we had the same amenities there that we'd had in Rawalpindi; guards at the gate to the house and a chauffeur to drive us places.

The north-eastern side of the town was bordered by hills, while the south-western part was composed of fertile plain with low hills strewn across it. As in some of the other cities in Pakistan, the summer season is extremely hot with a steep rise of temperature from May to June, during which time dust storms are frequent at night. Since we were arriving there in April, I assumed I'd see an occasional dust storm.

There were several trees scattered around our house; Jand and Mesquite trees and there were also lots of red poppy shrubs. I loved looking out my window at the Himalayan Cedars in the distance.

I grew to love our house and the area surrounding it. I'd had to transfer schools toward the end of the school year, but I quickly made friends with many of the young people in my school. I stopped being a tomboy and didn't play much with my brothers, as I would soon be sixteen.

Between April and September of that year, 1965, there was war with India concerning the area of Kashmir. I hoped that it wouldn't affect the entire nation of Pakistan. It seemed most of the damage was around the area of Lahore. I was glad we'd moved from Rawalpindi before the war actually started, because it is close to the Kashmir border. We all gathered around to listen to the news and, finally in September, 1965, a cease-fire was declared. Life in Pakistan would return to normal.

I celebrated my sixteenth birthday with excitement. I would graduate from high school at the end of the school year in 1966 and then planned to enroll in college. Since there were no colleges or universities in Mardan at that time, I decided to go to Peshawar University. It was only thirty miles away and I could easily go home for weekends and vacations.

CHAPTER FOUR

I had graduated from high school in 1966 at the age of 16. Our high schools only went to grade 10. We had to begin school at a young age and had only two months off every summer. I started college that fall just before my 17th birthday, the end of September. I enrolled at the Home Economics College which was part of the Peshawar University. It was strictly for girls. The only college at the University that had both genders was the Medical College.

Ecstatic that I was going to be living away from my family, I moved into a boarding house. I was set up with a room-mate, Zahida. She was my age and about the same size as me. However, she was just slightly taller. We got along right from the first day. We were conscientious about keeping the room clean and tidy. Our friendship blossomed and we became the best of friends.

Peshawar was a good university city and the Home Economics College was relatively new with emphasis on the sciences and different types of management. I signed up for all the classes I wanted and made sure to enroll in the drama club. I loved acting in plays and thought it was awesome, since I loved movies; especially those made in America.

I was excited to be back in the place of my birth, Peshawar. Although the town was surrounded by mountains on three sides and was situated in a valley, it did not receive the typical monsoon rains that other parts of Pakistan got. And therefore, normally, it got no relief from the scorching heat in summer. Since it was the end of summer, however, it wasn't quite as hot then.

I began making new friends there right away. They were mostly from prestigious families and suddenly, I started gaining more self-esteem. It seemed as though my professors loved me, and the young boys there always followed me, calling me nice names such as sweetheart.

Zahida and I were walking back to our boarding house one day and a boy from the University, whom we knew slightly, looked at me and said, "You're very beautiful." I was ecstatic when I realized he was looking straight at me.

"Thank you," I mumbled as my face turned a bright red. I wasn't yet used to people telling me I was beautiful, but I'd begun to believe them. Different boys had started following me around on campus and I heard they thought I was beautiful, too. My self-esteem was higher than it had ever been.

Many of my new friends were kind and thoughtful towards me, telling me I was beautiful, and I wished my abba could hear their assessment of me. Tears ran down my cheeks when I thought of how Abba had so totally ignored me and seemed not to notice that I existed. At least I now knew I was very pretty and didn't need anyone to tell me.

Some weekends, my abba would send the chauffeur to pick me up and drive me home to Mardan. That didn't happen too often though, only on certain weekends. However, most of the weekends, my friends and I would go to downtown Peshawar. We would walk around and eventually end up going to see an American movie; usually an Elvis Presley movie or something similar.

I was enjoying college and adapted quickly to a new way of life. I was learning so many new things, and it all seemed so exciting to me. I discovered I genuinely liked Biology and put forth a lot of effort to learn all I could. I especially enjoyed it when our Biology Professor would take us to the Medical College for lectures.

"We will be going to the Medical College today and I would like to prepare you for what you will be seeing," the professor announced after we had taken our seats in the classroom. She talked to us about the proper etiquette for visiting the Medical school, and then she led us on our excursion.

I was excited when we entered the Medical College and she led us to a room where there were dead bodies which they called cadavers. The smell of formaldehyde was a little bit overwhelming at first. I clamped my hand over my nose and glanced at Zahida who was doing the same thing. After listening to a lecture there, we headed back to our classroom across the campus.

About a month later, the professor took us back there to examine an assortment of bones in a laboratory. It seemed creepy, but still I liked learning all that I could.

I signed up to play on the girls' volleyball team and became quite good at it. Sometimes I would score more than other times. I loved sports and had developed a skill for it. It was exciting and fun every time I hit the ball over the net. Zahida was on my volleyball team and, after our games, we'd go home so excited we could barely concentrate on our homework. However, we knew we had to keep our grades up, or we wouldn't be allowed to play on the team.

Certain evenings every month, concerts were held at the boys' Engineering College, and all us girls were invited to attend. We girls would hike over to listen to the music which was being played. One of my favorite songs was 'Lipstick on Your Collar' by Connie

Francis. And of course, I loved everything Elvis; his music, his movies and his looks.

I loved to dance and did so every opportunity I got. Abba used to let us dance at his parties, and I was accustomed to it. One time when I was dancing, my Chemistry professor who disapproved came up to me and said, "Ambreen, you need to pay attention to your studies instead of dancing."

I wanted to tell her to mind her own business, but out of respect I lowered my head and walked out of the room. I ran into Zahida leaving the library. "Hey, I'm glad I found you," she said, walking toward me. "I wanted to know if you're interested in going to the concert tomorrow night."

"Sure," I said, perking up immediately. "I'm always interested in concerts. Do you know who's playing?"

"No, not really. I just heard a little about it and thought I'd like to go. Take a break from studying."

"I can't stay late though. I've got to rehearse my lines for the play. I have a big role and need to memorize all my lines as soon as possible," I said as we walked down the hall.

"I can listen to you while you practice," Zahida said. "Let's go home and hit the books, so we won't fall behind in our studies."

"Okay," I said as I hooked my arm in hers and headed toward the door. I was so happy to have Zahida to look out for me and include me in all she decided to do. Young and carefree, we were thoroughly enjoying our first year of college.

The following night we went to the Engineering College for the concert we'd been invited to attend. We swayed with the music and were caught up in all the excitement. The band played so many of my favorite tunes that when the concert ended, I continued to hum many of them on our way back to the boarding house where we lived.

I had finally memorized all the lines I needed to learn for the drama. The production was held the first week of spring. The play was reminiscent of a Shakespearean drama. I was told that my acting was terrific, and I felt I was walking home on clouds when I left the auditorium that night. There was a bouquet of flowers waiting for me when I got to the boarding house that night. It had been sent anonymously. My heart leaped to think someone thought enough of me and my acting to send beautiful flowers. I was moved to tears.

I would be going home to Mardan for a few days. It was hot that weekend with the temperature reaching 110 degrees. I was miserable from the heat and wanted to sit in front of a fan to cool off as soon as I walked in the door of our house.

The first thing I noticed was my father's young friend, Jamal. He was a local businessman who owned a factory that manufactured rugs and carpets; many of which were exported.

I was used to seeing him at our house frequently, since he used to visit there from time to time. Abba enjoyed his company, it seemed.

"Hi, Uncle Jamal," I said when I first noticed him. Even though he wasn't really my uncle, I called him that out of respect.

"Hello, Ambreen. I'm so glad you came home, so I can see you," he said, smiling. I looked away quickly because his smile was beginning to look like a leer. "Are you enjoying college?"

"Yes, very much," I said as I walked into the kitchen for a drink. When I returned to the living room, I saw Salima was there talking with Jamal. She had also come for a visit that weekend.

A bachelor of thirty years of age, Jamal was very rich, but not highly educated. His family was very religious, and belonged to a different sect than ours. Since there was no friction between the factions, we had no problems with those of his Wahhabi sect.

I sat down on a chair away from him. Something about the way he was following me with his eyes made me feel uncomfortable. I wasn't sure why he was paying so much attention to me when he'd been having a serious discussion with Salima when I came into the room.

Salima gave me a cursory glance before questioning Jamal. When she wanted to know something, she was relentless in her quest for the answers. "Why haven't you gotten married yet? What are you waiting for?" she asked, changing the subject they'd been discussing as she leaned forward on her chair and stared him in the eyes.

He shrugged his shoulders, so she continued talking. "Tell me the name of the girl you want to marry and I'll get her for you. Just write her name on my hand and leave the rest to me." She handed him a pen and held out her hand.

When he'd written on my sister's hand, she leaped off her chair and dashed to me, holding her palm open. "See, Ambreen. He wrote your name on my hand. He wants to marry you." She had an atrocious gleam in her eye as she looked at me.

I had a sinking feeling in the pit of my stomach. Even though I used to call him my uncle because he was so close to my abba, I wasn't that impressed with him. Yes, he was rich, but money wasn't that important to me. However, riches were very important to Salima. In fact, she was willing to barter me for some expensive jewelry. I didn't know it at the time, but he'd given her some grand jewelry she wanted while she worked at getting my father to agree to the marriage.

Tears sprang into my eyes and a lump formed in my throat. I felt as though I couldn't breathe for a moment. I got up and with my head down, I quickly left the room and barricaded myself in my bedroom. I didn't want to see or talk to anyone the rest of the evening. Not about to watch Salima manipulate Jamal, I refused to return to the living room even when she banged on my door and pleaded for me to join them.

It obviously didn't take her too long to convince my abba that I should be engaged right away. I stayed away from her and Abba the rest of the weekend and was happy to escape back to college. Abba reluctantly agreed with Salima that I would marry Jamal. I'm sure she manipulated my abba into setting the engagement in motion. I learned about the upcoming engagement ceremony after I'd returned to college. Abba called me and said, "You need to come home this next weekend. I have already engaged you to Jamal."

"Yes, Abba," was all I could say. I was speechless for a short while until after we hung up. I felt like screaming. It was just so unfair that I had been engaged to a man I didn't want to marry. Abba hadn't asked me if I was alright with marrying him. Jamal wasn't handsome like I'd hoped my future husband would be. He was just average looking, but one of the main reasons I didn't want to be married to him was because he was not an educated man. Education was so important to me and I had my heart set on marrying either a doctor or lawyer.

When I hung up the phone, I was weeping violently. Zahida came into our room just then and said, "Ambreen, what's wrong? Did someone die?"

It took me a full minute before I was able to answer her. "No, no one has died, yet. But I feel like I could die. I've been summoned home for the weekend. Would you go with me?" I asked Zahida. "You're my best friend and I could use your moral support."

"Yes, of course, I'll go with you. Why were you summoned home though?" Zahida asked with a serious look on her face. "Did something bad happen?"

"Yes and no. For my engagement," I mumbled and then began to cry even harder. I was sobbing so hard, I could barely breathe.

"Oh, my dear, I'm so sorry. I suppose it's the man you told me about who your sister wants you to marry," she said as she hugged me and wiped a tear off her arm.

I nodded my head yes and then threw myself on the bed and wept for quite some time until Zahida insisted I get up for dinner.

All through the meal, I pretended to eat, but only pushed the food around on my plate. I'd lost my appetite.

The days seemed to whiz by until the weekend. When the chauffeur arrived, we reluctantly went outside and climbed into the backseat of the car. He drove us to Mardan where everyone awaited my arrival.

When Zahida and I walked through the front door, Jamal was already there sitting with Abba. Both of them were talking loudly and laughing. I could hardly stand to look at either of them. I didn't want to marry Jamal. I didn't even want to be engaged to him. But I was stuck in a sticky situation and, like it or not, the engagement proceeded.

My ammi was sitting close by, and I could tell she was not happy about the engagement either. I looked at her face and saw the strain this decision had on her. Ammi had always told me she wanted me to only marry a man from our own sect of Islam. But she couldn't overrule Abba concerning the engagement. He had the final say.

I was sitting on a chair, not speaking to anyone. Jamal came over to me holding a ring in his hand and was ready to put it on my finger. I pulled my hand away from him, but he grabbed it and forced the ring on my finger. I didn't want to look at him, so I turned my face away. I was rendered utterly speechless. How could my family do this to me? Why couldn't I have a say in who I would marry? I wondered as tears filled my eyes and threatened to spill down my cheeks.

As soon as Jamal walked away, Zahida leaned over and whispered to me, "Ambreen, what are you doing accepting his ring? This is not the man for you. There are so many other men who would be better for you and you know it."

I felt the tears beginning to sting my eyes and I glanced away. "It's too late now and I had no input into the decision. I was not allowed to say no," I whispered back to my friend. "I'm already engaged." My heart felt like it had dropped into the pit of my stomach. I barely spoke to anyone the rest of that night.

Ammi came and gave me a hug. "I'm sorry, Ambreen," she whispered in my ear and then left the room. I noticed her eyes were sparkling with unshed tears.

As soon as I could, I headed back to college with Zahida. Jamal had already left for his house. I'm sure he was unhappy that I'd refused to talk to him over the weekend, but I really didn't care. Let him know how I'll treat him as his wife, I thought bitterly.

I was so despondent by the time we got back to the University that I could barely eat. Zahida worried over me like a mother hen. "Ambreen, you have to eat something. I'm so worried about you. If you don't eat, you'll die," she said to me one day when we were sitting at the dinner table, and I was pushing food around on my plate.

"Good, then I won't have to marry Jamal," I said, shooting her a defiant look as I got up and scrapped the food off my plate into the trash can.

"But then you won't be able to marry anyone else if you're dead, Ambreen," Zahida said, giving me a sympathetic look as she put her empty plate in the sink. "Please don't kill yourself over this engagement."

Most all of the time when I wasn't attending classes, I would cry ceaselessly. When I wasn't busy with school work, I walked around like a zombie. Zahida was so concerned about me that she wouldn't leave me alone for one minute of the day. She spent all her spare time trying to cheer me up even though I refused to smile at her.

I sat staring out the window of our room and didn't hear Zahida enter. She touched my shoulder and I jumped. "Are you alright?" she asked when I turned to look at her.

"No, I'm not. I'll never be alright as long as I'm engaged to Jamal. It's just not fair that I have to marry him," I replied with tears coursing down my cheeks.

At that point in time, I had no interest in anything, and life seemed so unfair. The thought occurred to me that Salima got to choose the life she wanted and marry the man she loved. Why couldn't it be that way for me also? I wondered.

CHAPTER FIVE

On a clear spring day, I received a message from Jamal. He was coming to Peshawar to visit me. I panicked and started flying around the boarding house, asking different girls if they would accompany me for ice cream when he arrived. Several of my friends said they would go with us.

"Zahida, if you see Jamal trying to get too close to me, pull me away, please. You know I don't want to be with him and I need help," I said as I opened my closet to see what I could wear.

"Don't worry," Zahida said as she sat down on her bed and watched me get an outfit out of the closet. I had selected the frumpiest, mismatched clothes I could find and put them on.

I didn't want him to look at me as desirable, so I pulled my hair back in an uncomely style and sat waiting for him to show up. Zahida commented to me that all my clothing was now too big on me. I didn't care. I didn't care how I looked, or what anyone thought of me. My depression was worsening, and there was nothing I could do to get out of it.

Jamal arrived promptly and I tried to pretend I was happy to see him. With a weak smile on my lips, I greeted him. "I'm hungry for ice cream. Could you take me and some of my friends to get some?" I tried to be as coy as possible, so he would agree. I didn't want to spend a minute talking with him, if I could avoid it. Having my friends with me would guarantee I'd be too consumed with conversation that I wouldn't have time for him.

Piling into the car, my friends all sat in the back. Reluctantly, I sat in the front passenger seat. I wouldn't look at him while he drove. At the ice cream parlor, I stayed in the car with my friends while he went in and purchased the ice cream.

Laden with a tray containing several cups of ice cream, he came back to the car. I did manage to get out and help him distribute the ice cream to the girls in the back seat. I took mine from his tray and slid back into the car.

He started the engine and pulled out of the lot. I took several big bites of my ice cream and then said, "Jamal, I'm not feeling very well now. I think the ice cream is making me sick. Can you take me back to our boarding house?" I asked, hoping he would just leave after dropping us off.

"I'm sorry you're sick. Maybe there's something wrong with the ice cream," Jamal said, looking at me with concern on his face.

I had feigned illness as a way to get rid of him, but he didn't seem to want to leave as he pulled up outside the boarding house and started to get out of the car.

"Really, Jamal, I think I just need to go to bed right now. I'm so sick I can hardly hold my head up," I said as I walked up the path to our boarding house. "Please, would you just go back home now and let me rest?"

"If that's what you want," Jamal said, a defeated look on his face. "I'll come another time and see you."

The girls and I entered the house and broke out into giggles as we heard his car start and drive off. I threw my half-eaten ice cream in the trash as I walked through the kitchen.

Later that evening, I was lying on my bed when Zahida stuck her head around the door frame. "Ambreen, I have some news to tell you."

I perked up and swung my feet over the side of the bed. "What?" I said. "Tell me what the news is about." I was very curious. By nature, I was a curious person and wanted to know everything going on around me.

"I was just on the phone talking to my brother and he told me something you should know about." Zahida had come into the room and was sitting on a chair close to my bed.

"So, don't keep me in suspense. Tell me what it is," I said as I smoothed my hair back from my face.

"Nadhir told me he knows Jamal and he's not the nice man some think he is. According to him, Jamal has been seeing a prostitute for some time. He thinks the woman is in love with Jamal and is upset that he's engaged now." Zahida clasped my hands in hers and squeezed.

"Oh, this is terrible," I said as a tear rolled down my cheek. In some ways, I wondered if it was good news. Maybe I could get out of marrying him; at least I hoped so.

The next time I went home, I was pleased to find out my father's youngest brother was staying there with the family. Chacha Bilal had always been one of my favorite relatives and was closer to my age than to my abba. He was always so nice to me and genuinely seemed to like me immensely.

At the first opportunity I got, I unloaded all my burdens on him, telling him about Jamal's other woman and how I never wanted to marry him anyway. It had only been Salima's ploy to get some expensive jewelry out of Jamal. When I finished telling

Chacha Bilal my story, he looked at me with sympathy and said, "I will talk to your abba and ask him to break the engagement.

"Thank you, Chacha," I uttered in a voice so low, I could barely hear it myself. Finally, someone in my family was listening to me and, with some luck, maybe I wouldn't have to marry Jamal after all.

Later that evening, I overheard my uncle telling my father about what he'd heard. "Jamal has been seeing a prostitute. Ambreen should not be obligated to marry him. He's not a good man anyway." I bravely walked into the room.

My abba exploded, "No. No, this is not a game where you can get engaged one day and the next day you break it just because you say you don't want to marry him." His face was red and he was glaring at me.

"Look at her, Bashir. She's going to die from starvation if you make her go through with this. She is so skinny now; her bones are all protruding. On the inside, she's sulking and has lost her will to live," Chacha Bilal said, pointing to me. "It's my opinion that you should stop this engagement."

After much bantering, Abba said, "Okay, the engagement is broken. I will let Jamal know right away." He gave me a stern glance and then nodded for me to leave the room.

I had already slipped the engagement ring off my finger and held it in my hand. "Thank you, Abba," I muttered as I dropped the ring in his palm and then left the room. I went straight to my bedroom and fell across the bed. Mixed feelings churned within me. Elated that I was free from Jamal, I was also scared that my abba would find another man even worse than him for me to marry. It took me a long time to go to sleep that night as I stewed over the possibilities of what might happen to me. Just before I dozed off, I came up with a plan that I would find someone like Salima did and force my abba into letting me marry the man of my dreams.

The unfortunate thing was that we were not allowed to have boyfriends. Somehow, I'd have to find a way to make someone love me; maybe a boy from my college. I'd have to work on my plan a while longer until I could finagle finding an ideal mate. My plan would have to remain secret for it to work.

I headed back to college with a new determination. I began to eat normal again and started to put on weight. My depression had already begun to lift and I had a new zest for life.

One morning Zahida sat across the table from me at breakfast and watched me consuming all the food on my plate. "You're beginning to look and act like the person I first met," she said as she cut a slice of apple in half.

"I feel like the person you first met," I replied and then laughed as I took the last bite of fruit on my plate.

The rest of the school year went by in a blur until summer vacation. I would be starting my second year of college in the fall and looked forward to going back to Peshawar University. But Abba had other plans.

"I'm being transferred to Lahore very soon," he said one morning when I joined the family at the breakfast table.

"Lahore?" I asked. "That's so far away. That means I'll have to stay at the boarding house all the time and won't be able to come home very often."

"I've given it some thought and I think you should transfer to Lahore University next year." Abba turned his head and continued to eat.

My ammi gave me a look of compassion. She knew I'd made a lot of friends at the University in Peshawar. "You'll make new friends at the University in Lahore," she said. "You can also keep in touch with your close friends from Peshawar." A faint smile crossed her lips.

Abba pointed out to us that Lahore had been a city known for its splendor under the Mughal Empire. Located in the north-eastern part of Pakistan near the India border, it was one of Pakistan's wealthiest cities. He also emphasized that Lahore was one of Pakistan's most liberal and cosmopolitan cities. Exerting a strong cultural influence over Pakistan, it was the major center for the publishing industry and literary scene. Also, the home to Pakistan's film industry, it seemed to have much to offer our family.

I began reading about Lahore in anticipation of moving there. I learned as much as I could about the major attractions such as the old Walled City and the Shalimar Gardens. I was beginning to relish the idea of living there.

I learned that the climate in Lahore is semi-arid with the hottest month being June. Temperatures can reach 104 degrees on average. It is also affected by the monsoon season which begins in late June. The wettest month of the year is July with its heavy rainfalls and evening thunderstorms. Cloudbursts are always possible, so driving can be tricky when they happen.

The move to Lahore took place sooner than I had thought it would. It would give me time to get my transfer to the University there and select my classes.

Our new house in Lahore was very large, also. It had seven bedrooms and the most lavish gardens around it. Before starting back to college, I spent much of my time sitting in the gardens and daydreaming about my future husband. He should be like Cinderella's Prince Charming; handsome and debonair, and he should also be a doctor or lawyer. Sitting under the Sufaid Kachnar tree which is also known as white orchid tree, I was pleased that we had moved after all.

CHAPTER SIX

Several months passed by while I concentrated on my school work. I had starting making good friends in Lahore, although Zahida and I did keep in touch and I still thought of her as my best friend. Overall, I had become quite happy and content.

I had joined the girls' tennis team and spent many hours practicing when I didn't have classes. We had a great team, and I was always thrilled when we beat the competition. It made me try even harder to become an expert at tennis.

I had been able to live at home, since the University was nearby. I was glad to spend time with Ammi after my classes and tennis games. My time after dinner was spent studying, so my grades would remain good.

One evening, as I emerged from my room where I'd been studying, Abba met me with a letter in his hand. "Ambreen, I need to talk to you," he said as he sat down on the sofa.

My heart nearly stopped. Now what have I done to upset him, I thought. My mind raced with all kinds of possibilities. I sat down on the sofa away from him and held my breath for a moment.

"Your Chacha Laeeq has sent a request asking for permission to engage his oldest son, Rashid, to you. I'm inclined to approve the engagement and marriage, since Salima defected and married someone else." Abba was sitting on the sofa with the letter held tightly in his hands.

My heart fell momentarily as I pondered the fact I would have to take Salima's place in a marriage to the man she betrayed. What could I say? As much as I wanted a good marriage, was marrying Salima's castoff the best deal for me?

Abba pulled a picture out of the envelope and shoved it in front of me. "Here's what he looks like now. I know you haven't seen him for many years, since he's been in the United States and England for quite some time."

I took the picture from Abba and stared at it. I instantly fell in love with his picture. He was so handsome with wavy, black hair and a thin moustache over full lips. He had kind, expressive eyes, too. "May I keep the picture, Abba?" I asked, holding it to my chest.

"Yes, of course. Does this mean you will agree to the marriage?"

"If he likes me, Abba, then I will agree to it," I said as I wondered if he would think I was pretty. Grateful that my abba had thought to ask my opinion before engaging me to someone else, I looked at him and smiled.

"Good, then I will invite him to come for a week and we can get things settled. I'm sure it will make Laeeq and Sheeba very happy to have him married to you," Abba said with a dismissive wave of his hand. "You know they were very disappointed when your sister broke the engagement to Rashid and married Mahmood instead."

"Yes, Abba. I'm sure they were. I'll try not to disappoint them," I said and then got up and walked back to my room. I felt like I was walking on air. I was going to be married to a handsome doctor who was living in the United States. Not only was he educated, but of our own sect in Islam. Salima's loss is my gain, I thought with a smile on my face.

It seemed like many months trudged by until I got the news that Rashid was going to be visiting us in Lahore. I was both excited and scared. What if he took one look at me and said no he wouldn't marry me? Things just had to go right for me for once in my life, I thought; and then I put the fears from my mind.

It happened to be the end of June, 1968, when Rashid finally came to visit us. My heart skipped a beat when I saw him walking through the gate toward the front door. He walked with his head downcast and I wondered if he was nervous, too. There was also a certain mysterious look about him, like he had some deep dark secret he was hiding. I passed it off as just his uneasiness over coming to acquire a new bride.

Zahid, Ali and Adnan all clambered around Rashid, talking and vying for his attention. He was so much older than them, but they had the utmost respect for our first cousin who had become a doctor and was living overseas.

"Tell us what it's like in America, Rashid," Adnan said, his dark eyes sparkling. A lock of black hair fell close to his left eye.

"It's very different from here," Rashid said. "The people there are more relaxed and their customs are so unlike ours."

"Will you tell us some details about it?" Ali asked as he joined in the conversation.

"I'll tell you all about the United States while I'm here," Rashid said. "Maybe someday you'd like to go see it for yourselves." He looked at all three of my brothers and smiled.

Abba and Ammi came into the living room and greeted him. We all sat around conversing and drinking tea. Looking at my brothers again, he began to delight us with tales of other lands; namely America and England. I'm not sure, but that may have been when my desire for travel and adventure took hold of me.

I was fascinated to learn of the various places in America where he had studied. First, he'd spent time in a state called Ohio, then New York City and finally, in Charleston, West Virginia. He had left there and gone to London for more studies, but had just returned to New York. He told us he was moving to a place called Brooklyn where he would be working at a Jewish hospital called Maimonides Medical Center.

I was very impressed with him and thought what a wonderful life I would have living with such an accomplished doctor. He was smart and worldly, so he could teach me about so many things I desired to know.

After a period of time we went into my room to talk more. Ali and Adnan joined us so we wouldn't be alone. We sat down on the chairs which were in my room. Rashid looked around the room and noticed a large poster of Elvis Presley that I had put up on my wall. He was a very famous singer from the United States and I loved listening to his songs.

Rashid asked, "Who's that in the poster?"

"You really don't know?" I asked. When he shook his head no, I answered, "Elvis Presley, the famous singer from America."

"Oh," is all he said and then suddenly, Rashid picked up a newspaper from a side table and opened it up to read after fumbling with it at first. I was surprised and said nothing. I became a little nervous and didn't know what to do, so I just sat quietly while my brothers talked.

Dinner was served and we were called to the dining table. Zareen had made quite the feast with all sorts of meat dishes and vegetables. An assortment of breads was on the table. Roti, also called chapati, is unleavened flat bread, whereas my favorite, naan, is made with yeast. I was happy to see both types.

Rashid took a chair close to mine and immediately began teasing me. First about the small amount of food I spooned onto my plate and then about how daintily I ate. I soon found it funny and began to laugh. By the time dessert was served, I was very much at ease and plunged my spoon into the rice pudding with certain gusto.

After dinner, Ali came up to me and said, "Ambreen, remember when we thought Rashid was reading the newspaper in your room?"

"Yes; why?"

"Well, I looked at the newspaper after Rashid put it down and he had torn a hole in the paper. We thought he was reading, when in reality he was watching you closely." Ali laughed so hard, I thought he was going to choke.

"That's odd, I admit, but maybe he wanted to see what I looked like when he thought I wasn't watching him," I said as I wondered why he'd do something so strange. However, I chalked it up to his nervousness at meeting me and making arrangements to marry.

As the days went by, I was beginning to feel comfortable around Rashid and looked forward to becoming his wife. I didn't want to say anything too soon, so as to give the impression I was in a hurry to get married.

The whole next week, Rashid teased me about first one thing and then another. I was already feeling comfortable around him and liked him immensely. At the end of the week, he informed us he would be returning to his parents' home in Karachi. I was sorry to see him go so soon.

Two weeks later, we were summoned to Karachi for the wedding ceremony. Since we'd be leaving in two days, Zareen called me into the kitchen and said, "Ambreen Bibi, you are not going to have servants in America and certainly no one is going to cook for you and your husband. At least not right now. Let me teach you how to make a couple of things, so you and Rashid won't starve or have to go out to restaurants to eat all the time."

I was grateful to her for attempting to teach me how to cook. With a lot of effort in those two days, I finally managed to make something that was at least somewhat palatable.

Finally, we left for Karachi. When we arrived at Rashid's family's home, we were informed the wedding was to take place the following day. It was a hasty marriage because Rashid had to return to the USA to start work. His parents had made all the arrangements for the wedding, including what I would wear.

My wedding dress was borrowed from my future sister-in-law. It was a pink and blue dress with gold embroidery woven throughout. I had my hair styled and make-up done and when I looked at myself in the mirror that day, I was pleased. I was somewhat disappointed that there was no time for a bridal henna party like Salima had had, but I consoled myself with the fact I was getting married and I didn't have to tolerate Salima's snide remarks to me. She and Mahmood had gone to England where he was taking some kind of army training.

My wedding was a small affair with only family members and close friends in attendance. The Maulana, a Muslim scholar known for his piety, who married us, thrust the papers at us. Rashid and I signed the marriage contract and then enjoyed the party to celebrate our union.

I was so happy to become Rashid's bride that I could hardly contain my excitement during the celebration. I kept looking at Rashid to see if he was as happy as I was, but couldn't read his expression well. I suppose it's because I don't know him very well yet, I thought, so I concentrated on thinking about our life together which should start soon.

In Pakistani culture, if the groom has no house or place to live, the family doesn't send the bride with him. And since the bride isn't going with the groom, there would be no wedding night to consummate the marriage. The rationale behind it was that if the girl got pregnant on the wedding night and the husband was somewhere else, it would be a hardship on the family as well as the wife. So, Rashid and I were kept apart that night, much to my chagrin.

Rashid left almost immediately to go back to New York. I would have to wait to go to the United States until he'd found an apartment to rent. As he was getting ready to leave for the airport, he put his arm around my shoulder and said, "I'll call you when it's appropriate for you to join me in New York."

"I'll wait for your call," I said, thinking it would be very soon. I watched him walk out the door with his suitcase and immediately began planning what all I should take with me when I went to America.

I returned to my family's home in Lahore and kept busy with reading novels and writing letters to Rashid. One day, a month later, I sat at my desk in my bedroom and daydreamed while looking out the window. It was the rainy season and the sky was almost black. Suddenly, my mood began to get as dark as the outdoors. I couldn't explain it, but when the torrential rains started, I felt tears forming in my eyes. I got up and flung myself across the bed. I realized my sadness was caused by not being able to go to my new husband yet.

When the school season began, I went back to college to finish getting my degree in history, a subject I loved. I had always loved sports, too and continued to play tennis that term. Each time I whacked the ball across the net, I felt I was taking out my frustration of having to live apart from my husband. Although the daily practices did help to keep my mind off Rashid's promise to take me to America.

That year slogged by so slowly I thought time was standing still for long stretches. I desperately wanted to go to America to join my new husband. We'd been denied a honeymoon and I felt somewhat cheated.

At least I'd started receiving letters from Rashid fairly regularly. Some were more informative about New York and his work; others proclaimed his love for me. 'I'm looking forward to you joining me here in New York, so I won't be so lonely without you,' he had written in more than one of his letters to me.

Many times, he would send small gifts. Some were sweaters; some were jewelry. He hinted in one of his letters that he'd purchased a ladies' watch for me, but he'd give it to me when I arrived in New York.

My heart soared each time I read his love letters. I felt sure he would ask me to go to New York any day in the near future. But months dragged by and still no invitation to join him. I was beginning to wonder why. Even Abba commented more than once about why I was still in Pakistan.

"I'm not sure why Rashid hasn't sent for me yet, Abba. Maybe his work is too intense right now for him to be able to help me get settled in America," I said, fearing that it was far from the truth, but I had no other explanations to offer. All Rashid's letters indicated it would be soon that he would call for me. I continued to hold onto the hope I had in my heart.

Finally, after a year had gone by, my abba talked to Rashid and told him he'd had adequate time to prepare for my joining him. He forced the issue and coerced Rashid into sending for me. At last, I would be going to America to join my husband. And although Rashid agreed for me to join him in New York, a new wrinkle developed. He said he'd been hospitalized and requested that I wait and come in the spring of 1970.

I was very disappointed that I would have to wait a while longer, but still I was excited that soon I'd be with Rashid and we could begin our life together. I went shopping to buy a lot of new clothing to take with me to America. Finally, I was ready for the new adventure in my life.

CHAPTER SEVEN

Abba made all the arrangements for my trip to New York. He procured my passport and visa as well as my airplane ticket. I had butterflies in the pit of my stomach as I was dropped off at the airport. "Goodbye, Ambreen," Abba said after helping get my suitcases out of the trunk. Our chauffeur was holding the door open for him. "Take good care of yourself and treat Rashid with respect. He's a good and honorable man."

"I will, Abba. Goodbye." I had mixed feelings as I told my father goodbye. I would miss my home, but would also welcome living in a new place with my husband.

I took my luggage to the British Airways counter and checked in. I was so nervous, I thought I would faint. My flight would take about 24 hours in total, changing planes twice. The second change would take place in London.

When it came time to board the plane, I followed others on and took my assigned seat near the back. They had given me a window seat and I glanced out while the plane was on the ground.

Not sure I wanted to see the ground falling away below us, I closed the window shade.

The engines started and seemed to rev for quite some time before we backed away and headed towards the runway. I was excited, but also scared as the plane roared down the runway and lifted off into the clouds. I didn't remember much of the first leg of the flight as I kept my eyes closed as much as possible. When the plane descended into Doha, Qatar, I felt that I could hardly move. I was jittery when I got off the plane and walked from one gate to the next.

Once I was on the next flight to London, I tried to relax. I read through the magazine that was in the back of the seat pocket. Too afraid to look out the window, I kept my eyes closed when I wasn't reading or eating the meals which we were served.

I had dozed off just before the plane started its descent into Heathrow airport. Startled awake, I thought we were crashing and closed my eyes even tighter. My fingernails were digging into the flesh of my palms.

When the plane landed, I gave a sigh of relief and when it was time to leave the plane, I was ecstatic to get off. I had cousins living in London and wished with all my might I could stay with them for a visit before boarding the next flight to New York City. But, of course, that was impossible. Rashid was in New York awaiting my arrival.

So, when the time came, I walked onto the jumbo jet with a spring in my step. I was one flight away from my husband and my new home.

All the way across the Atlantic Ocean, I daydreamed of what my new life would be like. I fantasized about my married life. Every scenario that I conjured up showed me as a contented wife with a loving husband.

As we were descending into New York, I could see the Statue of Liberty as we circled to land at Kennedy airport. Impressive looking, I wondered if we could visit it. I'd read so much about New York by that time, I knew of most places of interest, such as the Empire State Building and Times Square.

I left the plane and walked through customs and baggage. After retrieving my luggage, I wandered around for about forty-five minutes, looking for Rashid. I didn't leave the area for fear I would miss him, but he was nowhere to be seen. Almost feeling panicky, I wondered what I'd do if he failed to show up and get me from the airport.

Eventually, a Pakistani or Indian looking man walked up to me and said, "Are you Ambreen?"

"Yes, I am," I said as fear clutched my heart. Who was this man and why was he here instead of Rashid? I was even closer to panic at that time, when I noticed another man looking at us and smoking a cigarette.

"Oh, we've been looking for you for quite some time. Your husband is just over there," the man said, pointing to the one who was smoking.

When I looked back at the man who was smoking, I didn't recognize him. That's not Rashid, I thought to myself. The man had put out the cigarette and lit another one. He was looking away from us and seemed completely disinterested in his surroundings.

"Rashid," the man called to the smoking man. "Your bride is here, and we need to get home."

At that moment, I recognized Rashid as he crushed the cigarette in a tray and walked toward me. He held out his hand and shook mine. "Hello," he said.

His friend introduced himself as Mustafa. "My wife is cooking dinner for us, and I've asked Rashid if you and he would join us tonight. It will give my wife a chance to meet you, also." He motioned to Rashid to grab my luggage. "Come along."

We went out to the parking lot and got into Mustafa's car. When we arrived at his house, his wife was extremely warm and welcoming. Her name was Ammara and she seemed very sweet. "You must be tired, dear. Sit here while I put the food on the table," she said, hovering over me like a mother hen.

I was only twenty years old and had moved to a foreign country. I felt like I was living in some twilight zone at the moment. I couldn't understand Rashid's behavior toward me that day, or why we had to visit his friends on my first night in the USA. Granted, I was grateful for a good meal and sudden friendship, but I'd rather have gone to Rashid's apartment and rested for the evening.

After several hours of attempting to keep myself awake, Mustafa looked at me with sympathetic eyes and said to Rashid, "Why don't you take your wife home, so she can rest? She's had a very long flight here and must be exhausted."

"Oh, okay," Rashid said as if it hadn't occurred to him that I might need to rest. He helped me up and walked me to the front door. "Goodnight. Thanks for taking me to the airport, and for dinner."

Mustafa and Ammara stood in the doorway and waved goodbye to us as we went to Rashid's car. He held the door for me while I got in and then put my luggage in the trunk. When he slid into the driver's seat, he looked at me and said, "How do you like my new car? I just bought it a few weeks ago."

"It looks nice," I said, not really caring about the car. I was so sleepy; I was barely aware of my surroundings until Rashid pulled the car up in front of the apartment building and parked in the last available parking spot. As we got out of the car, I noticed the front of the hospital across the street. That must be Rashid's workplace, I thought as I waited for him to get my luggage and then followed him through the door of the building.

We entered the elevator and as soon as the door shut, Rashid said, "It will go up now." I looked at him like he was crazy. Did he think I was from some remote village and didn't know what an elevator was?

I just closed my eyes and waited for the elevator door to open, and then followed him down the hall. Rashid opened the door to his apartment and let me enter first. It was a small furnished one-bedroom unit and it looked somewhat tidy at first glance. I went to the bathroom while he took my suitcases to the bedroom. As soon as I came out and stood in the doorway of the bedroom, I saw him kick the twin beds apart. They had been pushed together to appear that it was one full-size bed. The one on the outside landed at an angle. He looked at me and pointed to the angled bed. "This one is your bed," he said. "You must be very tired. You can go to sleep now." I felt he was treating me like an intruder in his apartment and in his life.

As soon as he left the room, I sat down on the bed he indicated would be mine. Soon, he came back with a pill and a cup of water in his hands. "This will make you feel comfortable and you'll sleep very well." He held them out for me to take.

I took it from him and swallowed the pill. Feeling so confused by his strange behavior, I couldn't talk to him that night, so I got ready and went to bed. Soon, I was fast asleep.

When I awoke the next morning, he had already prepared hot cereal and tea for me. He pulled out a chair at the kitchen table and I sat down and began eating. He was already dressed and ready for work by then.

Pointing to the refrigerator, he said, "You can have anything you want. There's also some food in the cupboards. I have to leave for work now, but here's my phone number if you need to reach me." He thrust a small sheet of paper at me. "Don't worry. I'll be back later today."

"Okay, thanks," I said, still feeling very tired from my long, arduous trip the previous two days. More than anything, I just wanted to rest and relax for a day or two, but I knew I couldn't do that since I had much to do.

After he left, I felt glad for the opportunity to be alone while I unpacked my belongings and put things in order. Although I was very surprised that he didn't even take one day off from work to be with me on my first day in America. Brushing those feelings aside, I busied myself with getting settled into my new home and almost didn't hear the telephone ringing.

I rushed to pick up the receiver. "Hello," I said, a little out of breath.

"Hello. Who is this?" a woman's voice asked. She definitely had an American accent.

"I am Mrs. Ahmed," I replied as I wondered who this woman could be.

"So am I," she said. "I'm Shelly Ahmed, Rashid's first wife. Is he there?"

Rashid's wife? My brain couldn't comprehend this. Why was this woman saying that?

"No, he's at the hospital right now and won't be home until later tonight," I muttered as I fell back onto a chair. My legs had become weak and couldn't hold me upright.

"Please tell him I've not received the check yet and that it's two weeks late," she said. "He did tell you about me, didn't he?"

"No, he didn't." I was in a complete state of shock at that time. I didn't know what more to say. It felt as though someone had thrust a dagger through my heart. My body felt numb.

"Rashid and I were married and our divorce was only final a few weeks ago," Shelly said. "He told me his father disapproved of our marriage and he was ordered to divorce me. I'm surprised he didn't tell you about me. According to what Rashid told me, his parents arranged for him to marry you. I don't remember your name though."

"Ambreen," I said. Suddenly, things were falling into place. It now made sense why he'd left me in Pakistan for so long after our wedding. He needed to divorce his other wife before he could bring me to America. I knew enough about the law of the land to know that you couldn't have more than one wife in the United States. It was considered a crime.

My brain had stopped working. I don't know what else this woman said because my mind had stopped processing what she was saying. Finally, she hung up, and I went to the bathroom and was hitting my head against the walls. I cried and cried for so long that I thought I shouldn't have any tears left. I wanted the soothing presence of my ammi, but she was half a world away in Pakistan. I flung myself across the bed and continued crying until finally, I must have dozed off.

Evening fell and Rashid returned to the apartment. When he walked into the living room where I was standing with my arms folded, I blurted out, "Your wife called. I didn't know you were married. Why didn't you tell me?"

Rashid's face turned bright red with embarrassment as he came towards me. Taking both my hands inside his, he said, "Come here. I have to talk to you." He led me to the sofa and made me sit, and then he sat down beside me and said, "You are very beautiful and anybody would be lucky to marry you, but the timing was wrong. I was already married to Shelly Sinclair." He stopped as though that explained everything. I had a questioning look on my face, so he continued, "When I first came to the USA, my father told me to never look at the girls here. He said to always think about God, pray and keep my eyes downcast. Always write and read the holy book."

I was listening to Rashid, but nothing he was saying was making any sense. He was not yet telling me important details about his marriage to his ex-wife, Shelly. I sat patiently waiting for him to finish explaining.

He looked away for a few moments and then said, "When I was younger, my doctor friends all had girlfriends or wives. Some of them were making fun of me and asking if I was gay. They asked me why I didn't have a girlfriend. I couldn't explain anything to them, because this environment is so different from ours. So, they found a girl for me. She was a nurse and we got together. I had no idea you existed in Pakistan. I mean, I knew you were my cousin, but I remembered you as being very, very young. My parents never told me there was a girl named Ambreen that I would have to marry."

"So, your parents knew you were married, but didn't tell me. I feel like I've been lied to by the entire family," I said with a whimper, wondering if my own family knew of Rashid's marriage in America. "So, you've still not told me how you ended up married to her."

"I got involved with Shelly and then her mother wanted her to marry, because she came from an old-fashioned family, too. So, I married her. When I told my father about it, he started demanding that I divorce her immediately. He told me he'd commit suicide if I didn't divorce Shelly and marry Ambreen. He also said nobody would marry my brothers or sisters and that people in Pakistan would think I was not a good person."

This was a lot to take in. I was surprised to hear that Chacha Laeeq would use emotional blackmail. But then I'd been surprised by a lot of things lately.

Rashid rambled on for quite some time and, although I tried to absorb everything he said, I was emotionally drained and, for a time was mentally disconnected. Then he put his arm around my shoulder and said, "I promise I will always take good care of you and maybe someday we will both fall in love with each other."

In cultures where marriages are arranged, the husband and wife usually fall in love with each other after they've been living together for some time. Just then, I questioned if we would ever fall in love. I wondered if he still loved Shelly. He must have loved her to have married her, I thought. The possibility that he still did was very high. The love I thought I'd felt for Rashid's handsome face when looking at his picture vanished that day. Now, as I glared at him, I considered that I had been only foolish.

I tried to stay away from him and eventually we ended up living like brother and sister for a period of time. He started calling me 'kid'.

A few days passed and I kept myself busy, cleaning and doing laundry. I decided to change the sheets on the beds. I threw back the covers and found a light-colored hair pin in one of the beds. I picked it up and stared at it. Shelly must have been here, I thought as tears rolled down my cheeks.

The second week I was in New York, Rashid's boss, Dr. Stevens, called. "How are you doing, Ambreen," he asked when I answered the telephone and he'd identified himself.

"I'm fine," I said, wondering why he was calling me. My first thought was that something had happened to Rashid at work.

"How do you like the USA?"

"Very good," I replied, relieved that the call wasn't about my husband.

"My wife and I would like to invite you and Rashid to dinner tomorrow night," Dr. Stevens said. "I do hope you can come, so we can get acquainted with you."

"I'm sure it will be fine with Rashid," I said and told him goodbye.

The next evening, Rashid and I went to dinner at the Stevens' house. When we walked in, Dr. Stevens said, "I'm so happy for the opportunity to get to know you." He took my coat from me and held out his hand for Rashid's coat.

Before I could open my mouth to respond, Rashid said, "She can't speak English." I was stunned. How could he say that?

"I'm very surprised," Dr. Stevens said, looking at me. "When I was on the phone with her, she was very comfortable speaking

English." He turned toward Rashid, "How can you say she cannot speak English now?"

Rashid cast his eyes downward and didn't answer. I saw that Dr. and Mrs. Stevens were looking at each other and shrugging their shoulders.

I was so insulted that he wouldn't let me speak that I didn't say a word the whole evening. Embarrassed by the whole event, I couldn't look at either Dr. or Mrs. Stevens.

A week later, Rasid called me from work and said, "Dress nicely and pack an overnight bag. I've decided to take you to Washington, D.C."

I had still not forgiven him for deceiving me, but I'd heard so much about Washington, D.C. that I became excited to visit there and see the monuments. Hopefully, it would also give me a chance to visit with my aunt who lived there.

I scoured through the closet and found one of my prettiest outfits. Hastily, I packed a bag to take with me. I was ready and waiting when Rashid walked in the front door.

I didn't talk at all on the drive to D.C. Rashid kept up a running monologue about the different places we passed through. I had tuned him out and only said things like huh or uh huh on occasions to make him think I was interested in what he had to say.

He drove us straight to the mosque in D.C. I marveled that he knew where it was located. Obviously, he'd been there before, but he'd never mentioned going there in the past.

We got out of the car and walked to the entrance. Slipping our shoes off, we walked inside where Rashid immediately told an imam that we were there to get married. He explained we'd had a quick wedding in Pakistan, but felt we should marry in the United States.

I was flabbergasted. I had no idea he was taking me to get married again. The thought occurred to me as I stood there waiting that since he'd been married to Shelly at the time of our Pakistani wedding, he thought maybe it hadn't been a real marriage. And probably in the eyes of the United States it hadn't been.

Of course, in my country it was legal to have more than one wife. Although polygamy is legal there, it is restricted. Only males adhering to the Islamic faith are allowed up to four wives at any one time. They're required to obtain legal consent from their current wives and must show they have the ability to properly take care of all of them.

I stood there glaring at Rashid. If he thought this wedding was going to cause me to start living with him as a wife, he had another think coming. I was not ready to forgive him.

Soon the imam began the ceremony to unite us in matrimony, again. I repeated the necessary words and at the end of them, I began to feel the ice in my heart start to melt. Maybe I could forgive him and live as his wife. Just not yet, however.

As soon as we walked outside the mosque, we put our shoes on and got in the car. When Rashid started the engine, I turned to him and said, "Why don't we visit my aunt here for a few days. We could tour some of the monuments here in D.C. I'd really like to see them," I said, hoping he'd agree to stay. I hadn't really been talking to him and didn't think to tell him ahead of time that I'd like to visit her.

"Okay, we can stay with your aunt for a couple of days," Rashid said as he pulled the car away from the curb. "Tell me her address."

My aunt was happy to see us and we stayed at her house for three nights before going back to New York. During that time, Rashid took me to see the Washington and Lincoln monuments as well as the White House and the Smithsonian Institute. I was very impressed with Washington, D.C.

When we arrived back in Brooklyn, things went back to the way they were. We were still living like siblings and he was still calling me 'kid'. He started taking me to watch Indian movies. I believe he did that to appease me, so I wouldn't think about his deceitfulness.

One night I was getting ready for bed and Rashid came into the bedroom and looked into my eyes. He took hold of my shoulders and said, "Your eyes and forehead look so much like Shelly's."

I was utterly stunned. I couldn't believe he would dare to compare my features to hers. I narrowed my eyes as I glared at him in contempt. "And just how do you think our eyes are alike?" I asked in a spiteful tone, fury rising within me.

"You both have big eyes," Rashid said with a smile on his face. He could see nothing wrong with telling me this. Funny, I thought, now that I know about Shelly, he's willing to bring her up and tell me things about her features.

Now I had to worry that every time he looked at me, he would see Shelly. Was my life always going to revolve around her? I wondered how long I would be able to tolerate it all.

When we awoke the next morning, I didn't even bother to say anything to him. I was still so angry. I didn't know why he was treating me like that. Had he treated Shelly in a similar manner? I questioned. Had he compared her to someone else? Probably not, I concluded.

I ate my breakfast in silence. He ate quickly and left for work. As soon as he walked out the door, I started cleaning the kitchen from top to bottom. Being furious seemed to give me a little extra strength and soon the kitchen was polished to a gleam. By the time I was finished, some of the anger had abated and I was feeling better.

I thought quite a lot about Shelly, especially when I was at home alone. Every day when he went to work, I would wonder if Shelly had come to New York and was meeting Rashid. Were they working together? Were they laughing and having a good time while I was sitting at home feeling depressed? The jealousy was beginning to get to me, and I couldn't get the situation out of my head.

On a chilly Saturday morning in early May, Rashid urged me to get out of bed and get dressed. "Hurry and get up, kid. Let's go out for breakfast and then go to the Statue of Liberty. After that, we can take the elevators to the top of the Empire State building."

"I'd like to see them," I said as I pulled on my clothes and grabbed my purse.

Our first stop was at a small restaurant where we ate our breakfast. Then we took the ferry across to Liberty Island. "Can we go all the way to the top?" I asked Rashid as we got off and walked toward the statue.

"Yes, but the elevator only goes to the top of the base, and then you have to climb the stairs all the way up. Are you able to do that?"

"I hope so. If not, we can come back down, can't we," I said, hoping to make it to the top.

"I think so," he said as he glanced up at the statue. "If I remember correctly, there are platforms where you can rest while climbing to the top. I think we had to stop for a minute last time I was here."

I mulled over his last statement; the last time he was here, they had to stop for a minute? Who was he referring to? Shelly? I didn't want to ask him and ruin the day by knowing he'd brought her here, too.

We entered and began the slow ascent to the top. We had to stop several times, but it was exhilarating to be able to look out of the crown. Afterwards, we went to the Empire State building and took the elevators to the top. Standing there looking out over New York City, I forgot about the miseries I'd recently endured, at least for a minute or two.

When we got back to the apartment, I decided I wanted to make something special for dinner. I had already begun to experiment with cooking. I remembered what Zareen had taught me in those two short lessons before I got married and put them into practice. I bought a cookbook and started following recipes. I was having fun making all sorts of delectable dishes for us. On more than one occasion, Rashid had commented that I was becoming a very good cook.

When the food was ready, we sat at the table to eat. "This is really delicious, Ambreen," Rashid said as he lifted another chicken leg off the platter.

"I'm glad you like it," I said, feeling proud of accomplishing something worthwhile. I cut into the chicken breast that was on my plate and took a bite.

Over the months I'd lived in Brooklyn, I had made friends with some of the other doctors' wives and it helped me to remain sane. I went places with them to shop or have lunch. I learned a great deal from them and was so glad to have friends I could spend time with. However, I couldn't confide my deepest feelings to them as I didn't want them to know about Rashid's intriguing past.

CHAPTER EIGHT

A couple of months passed and another emotional bomb was dropped. I felt like my head was going to explode. I was blown away again with more unexpected news.

"Hello," I said as I picked up the phone.

"Hi, Ambreen. Would you please tell Rashid that I've not received the money he owes me? Let him know that I desperately need it and would like him to send it right away," Shelly said when I answered the phone. I was still very confused about the money Rashid owed Shelly. Why does he owe her money, I wondered? Is it just because he was married to her?

"I'll let Rashid know," I said, contemplating why she was desperate for money from him, since she was a nurse and was probably working.

"Thanks. So how do you like living here in America now, Ambreen?" she asked.

"I would like anywhere in the world, if I knew I was loved," I replied as a feeling of hurt came over me. "But I don't think Rashid loves me. I think he still loves you. Sometimes he just sits and stares into space and I'm sure he must be thinking about you."

"Oh, I'm sure he loves you now and not me," Shelly said. "We were apart for some time, and I'm sure he stopped loving me."

"If I'd known he was married to you, I never would have married him," I said. "But that fact was kept from me the entire time, until I learned about it from you."

"I'm sorry no one told you, Ambreen," Shelly said, sympathy in her voice. "It wasn't right for them to withhold that kind of information from you."

Just then I heard a child's voice in the background. "Is there a child there with you?" I asked. "Is that your child?" Hope sprung in my heart that Shelly had remarried someone else and had a child by him. I didn't think about the fact that she'd said Rashid and she were just divorced weeks before I arrived.

"Yes, it's our daughter, Anita; mine and Rashid's daughter. The money he's supposed to send is for her care. I have to have her in a nursery school while I work and it's quite expensive."

You could have knocked me over with a feather. Another thing I had not been informed about. Rashid had admitted he'd been married to Shelly, but failed to tell me about their daughter.

"Would you send me a picture of her? But don't send it to this address. I'll give you one where Rashid won't see that you've written or sent a picture. I'll send it back to you," I said. I was so curious to see this little girl that belonged to my husband. The thought occurred to me that I'd be able to tell if it was really his child or not. Maybe Rashid wasn't sending the money regularly because he thought the child wasn't his.

"Sure, I'll send you a picture of Anita. She's really a beautiful little girl," Shelly said, bragging about her daughter's looks.

I gave her my friend's address. She lived next door and wouldn't mind my using her mailbox.

A few days later, I received a letter from Shelly. Inside was a picture of Anita in the arms of her father, Rashid. There was no doubt that she was his daughter. She resembled him with her dark hair that was pulled up in pig tails and big dark brown eyes. She looked to be about three years old. I wondered if Shelly sensed that I questioned if her child was really Rashid's and so sent one with him holding her.

The letter that Shelly wrote was very kind. I thought if we'd met in a different time and place, under different circumstances, I may have really liked her.

I hadn't said anything to him after Shelly called. I'd wanted to wait until I received the picture and knew for sure if Anita was his daughter before I said anything to him. The time had come to let him know that I knew.

I was waiting on Rashid to come home from work. Sitting on the sofa with my arms folded, I greeted him with a glare that told him something was wrong once again. Before he had a chance to settle into a chair, I lit into him.

"Why didn't you tell me you and Shelly had a daughter? Why do I always have to find things out from her when she calls to say you're late with the child support payment?"

He started making excuses and finally just admitted that he and Shelly had a daughter. "I know I should have told you, but I was afraid to upset you any more than you already were," Rashid said, walking to a different chair opposite me. Sitting down, he kept his eyes downcast and folded his hands on his lap.

"I'm your wife now, Rashid. You should have been honest with me and told the entire story in the beginning. Is there anything else I don't know about that I may find out later on?" I asked, staring straight at him.

"No, there's nothing else to tell you now," Rashid said, looking very humble as he glanced at me and then looked away.

When I sent the picture back to Shelly, I thanked her for sending it and told her that Rashid had finally admitted he had a daughter with her. I included a picture of myself in the hopes she would send me one of her. I selected a flattering picture that made me look very pretty. I hoped that it would make her as jealous of me as I was of her. However, I never received a picture of Shelly.

The next time I wrote to her, I let her know just how close Rashid and I were getting and hinted that we were very much in love. Although it wasn't really true, I hoped it would make her want to leave him alone and not bother to ask for child support. I wasn't sure what it was all about anyway; were fathers supposed to send money to their ex-wives forever? Since I never knew anyone who was divorced with children, I wasn't sure what the father's duty was toward his child.

Shelly and I wrote to each other for a short period of time. I suppose it was ultimately jealousy that caused us to stop staying in touch. If I could keep her and their daughter off my mind, I would find it easier to be a real wife to Rashid. After all, I surmised, it wasn't my fault their marriage broke up.

I hinted to Rashid that I needed a new watch, thinking maybe he'd give me the one he'd let me believe he had bought for me while I was still in Pakistan. "I'll take you out and buy a new one for you," Rashid said, glancing up from his medical journal.

The following day, he took me to a department store and let me pick out a nice watch. I wondered about the one he indicated he already had for me. Maybe he gave it to Shelly, I thought, but said nothing about it.

Over the next few months, I noticed how paranoid Rashid was becoming. It seemed he was afraid of his own shadow at times. His behavior was more than just a little weird, and I didn't know how to deal with it.

One night as we sat in the living room watching a television show, a shampoo commercial came on. He said, "Do you understand this shampoo? It means they want to cut off my head. They're trying to tell me indirectly that they'll come and cut off my head." I could see the fear in his eyes when I glanced over at him.

"Rashid, shampoo is for cleaning your hair," I said as I looked at him in astonishment. "Where did you get the idea it's because someone wants to cut off your head?"

"They must have hired you to kill me," he said, moving away from me on the sofa and holding his hands around his head. He looked so frightened that I actually felt I should be protecting him from some unknown menace.

I was beginning to wonder about his mental stability. He never said anything about mental problems, but something wasn't right, I'd noticed. I made the decision to start paying very close attention to his actions. I wished I'd asked Shelly about it while we were still writing to each other. She may know what's wrong with him, I thought.

Rashid had begun saying some very weird things about people wanting to kill him. I didn't know why he appeared so obsessed about it and for the most part, I tried not to dwell on it. I was afraid it would send me over the edge and make me crazy, too.

Sometimes I would come home from shopping with my friend and find Rashid hiding behind the couch. He wouldn't want to come out until he was certain no one else was in the apartment except us. I would sit beside him at times to make him feel more comfortable.

It had been raining earlier in the day, but had stopped. Rashid wanted to go out to eat at his favorite Indian restaurant that evening. When we got on the elevator, there was an old woman standing toward the back, holding her umbrella.

When she got off on the next floor, he said, "Did you see that? She was holding a gun." He had a look of fear on his face.

"No, it was an umbrella," I replied as the door opened and we stepped off.

"You're going to lie to me, too?" Rashid said in anger. He was glaring at me and his eyes were bulging. "Why can't you ever believe me when I tell you someone wants to kill me?"

"Okay, Rashid, I believe you," I said, turning away to walk out the door. I didn't want to argue with him over something so unbelievably ridiculous. What's going on with him, I wondered. Something wasn't right, but I didn't know what it was. And I didn't know how to help him with it.

CHAPTER NINE

Toward the end of November, 1970, Rashid came home one day and said, "I think we need to move to Canada. The United States is against me because I married Shelly who's a Christian woman, and I divorced her to marry a Muslim girl. All the American people hate me. They'll try to kill me," he said almost in a whisper.

"They're not trying to kill you, Rashid," I said, feeling a little perturbed. I was getting tired of his incessant talk about persecution.

He glared at me with a look of malice I'd never noticed before. "You don't know anything about it, so be quiet. We will move to Canada as soon as possible. I can't live here any longer."

I knew essentially nothing about Canada, so I wasn't too excited to move there. I knew his sister had gone to the Province of Alberta in Canada and lived in a town called Calgary, but it was somewhere in the Western part of Canada. I asked Rashid if we were going there and he said no. He thought Ottawa might be a good place to go. So, plans were made for our move to Ottawa.

Situated on the south bank of the Ottawa River, it is also at the confluence of three major rivers. The Rideau Canal, off of the Rideau River, forms the world's largest skating rink in the winter. I thought I might like to try ice skating there, if I could convince Rashid to take me.

In December, Rashid found an apartment close to the hospital in Ottawa, and so we packed our few belongings and moved there. Since his apartment was furnished, we had no furniture to move. We loaded our things into the car and drove to Canada.

"I hope you'll be happy in Ottawa," I said as we drove into the city limits. "It will give us a fresh start here." I hoped putting distance between him and Shelly would ease his mind and he would recover from whatever mental malady he had developed.

Once we were settled into our place, he starting saying we should stop living like friends and become real husband and wife. "If you have children, it will bring us closer," he said to me one evening after we'd finished dinner. "And maybe we'll have a loving relationship then."

"Do you want more children, Rashid?" I asked, thinking about his other daughter, Anita, whom he never saw.

"Yes, I think it would be good for us to have them," he replied, a grin on his face.

I thought maybe he was right and so in late January we began to live like a married couple. In March, I became pregnant with our first child. Rashid seemed to be pleased that we would have a child of our own.

At first, I thought maybe the move to Ottawa had been just the thing he needed, and he did seem alright for a time. But shortly after I got pregnant, he started saying things about Shelly sending people against him. It seemed she was deeply rooted in his mind, and he couldn't get her out. But just as quickly as he'd started saying that, he stopped, and I thought he was going back to being normal again.

One day, I walked into the room and he was talking on the telephone and I heard him say, "You promised me you would not call. Why are you calling?" When he noticed me, he waved me away; urging me out of the room. He had a frown on his face and looked embarrassed.

I just assumed it was Shelly and she was harassing him. Of course, when he hung up, he refused to talk about it or tell me who was on the phone with him. He was shutting me out again. I felt isolated and lonely. I started looking for female friends.

While in Ottawa, I did make a lot of friends and enjoyed socializing with them. I was beginning to feel like we were going to have a normal life after all. Overall, Rashid did seem more normal in some ways than he had in Brooklyn. My hopes soared and I thought maybe the fact that we were going to have a child had had a real impact on Rashid. Maybe life in Canada would be better than in the United States where Shelly lived.

One day, our friends, a Pakistani couple, invited us to a dinner party. We accepted the invitation and went to their house. The host as well as all the male guests were doctors and most were from Pakistan. One of the doctors was from Afghanistan. Everyone brought their wives to the party.

We mingled and talked to most of the guests and then the doctor from Afghanistan starting talking to me in Pashto, which is the language of Afghanistan. I could speak it, since some of our servants spoke that language. I'd learned to speak four different languages, including English as I was growing up. I'm not sure how he knew I'd understand him, but when he talked I answered him in the same tongue.

Rashid thought we were talking about him. He grabbed me by the arm, pulling me to my feet and said, "Let's go now." He had an angry look on his face.

"What are you doing?" I asked him as he dragged me from the room. As soon as he got me outside, he flung open the car door and shoved me inside. He got in the driver's seat, started the engine and drove us back to our apartment.

As soon as we got home, he locked the door and put the chain on to further secure it. "Go put on your pajamas," he ordered, pointing me toward the bedroom. I complied, walked in and changed out of my clothes and into a thin night gown. At four months pregnant, I was already beginning to show by then.

All of our friends from the party were horrified about the incident and had followed us home. Everyone except the doctor from Afghanistan came to our apartment. We heard a knock on the door and someone said, "Rashid, it's okay. We're not going to bother you, but please send Ambreen out. We'll take her and you can stay here." I recognized the voice of our host.

"No," Rashid answered, an angry countenance on his face. "I will not send her out."

A half hour later, there was a loud knock at the door and someone said, "Hey, Dr. Ahmed, it's the police. Please, you have to open the door; otherwise, we have to break it."

Rashid grabbed me by the arm and dragged me to the door. He removed the chain, undid the deadbolt and opened the door, shoving me out into the hall. I was appalled by his action. There I stood in my thin nightgown, bare legs showing and I was so embarrassed I could have died.

In Muslim culture, a woman should not go around other Muslim people without covering her legs. One of the ladies was wearing a dopata, which is a large scarf. She took it off and covered my legs with it. I was grateful that I had something to hide my legs as I stood in the hallway.

After Rashid had shoved me into the hall, he'd put the chain back on the door again. The police knocked once more and told him to open the door. Still he wouldn't open for them, so they broke the chain and forced their way in.

I had been taken into an apartment next door where one of my friends lived. We were watching from the doorway and saw them lead Rashid out of our apartment. They stopped and talked to me. "We're taking him to the hospital to have him admitted to the mental ward. I suggest you get dressed and have someone drive you there. You'll need to help with the paperwork, so he can be admitted."

"I'll be right there," I said as I made a mad dash for our apartment and quickly changed into regular clothes. My friends drove me to the hospital. He was being admitted to the mental ward of the same hospital where he had been working.

It dawned on me that perhaps our host had seen signs of mental instability in Rashid at the hospital and this incident was just the straw that broke the camel's back, so to speak.

I called Rashid's sister, Jabeen, who lived in Calgary and begged her to come help me. "Please come to Ottawa," I said when she answered the phone. "Something awful has happened to Rashid, and he's in the hospital. I need you to come here and help me, please." I poured out my heart to her, so she would know how all alone and helpless I felt. Here I was half way around the world from my family, my husband in a mental facility, and I didn't know what to do.

"I'll make arrangements and be there as soon as I can," Jabeen said. "I can probably be there by tomorrow."

"Thanks," I said and then hung up the phone.

I had a sudden urge to call Shelly and talk to her about his mental problems. She probably knew him fairly well and might have some insight into his problem. I dialed her number and when she answered the phone I said, "Shelly, I just want to let you know Rashid has been admitted to the hospital. He was out of his mind. I think he has some mental illness." I didn't know what his diagnosis was at that time.

"I'm sorry to hear that," Shelly said, her voice had an edge of kindness to it. "He told me that before he came to see me and file for a divorce in the fall of 1969, he'd been hospitalized in a mental ward. He told me that he'd been diagnosed with paranoid schizophrenia."

"Do you know what caused him to develop it?" I asked as tears rolled down my cheeks.

"No. I have no idea what caused him to develop it," Shelly said. "It's hereditary, I think."

"Did he have symptoms of it when you and he were together?" I asked.

"No, he was perfectly sane when we were together. He must have developed it sometime after he left me and before he came to file for divorce."

We talked a few more minutes before hanging up. I was glad I'd called Shelly, but I didn't have any definite answers. I wasn't sure what paranoid schizophrenia meant, but intended to find out. Shelly denied being in touch with him, like I'd thought. I still wanted to believe she was the cause of his mental illness, because it made me feel better to have someone else to blame.

Jabeen rushed to Ottawa to help me and I was so grateful. I picked her up from the airport and drove to our apartment. As soon as she got her things unpacked, we left for the hospital to see him. When I walked through the door into his room, I almost cried. They had him in restraints, because they said he'd been belligerent and had tried to escape.

I went over to him and kissed him on the cheek. He gave me a smirk and then turned his head away. A nurse was checking his vital signs, so Jabeen and I sat down in the chairs closest to his bed.

Jabeen tried to talk to him, but he tuned her out and wouldn't look at us again. While we sat there not knowing what to do, his doctor came in. His name tag read, Dr. Lee, and he looked Chinese.

Dr. Lee asked us to leave the room while he examined Rashid and talked with him. Jabeen and I went into the waiting room and sat down. Neither of us said anything. We were distressed that Rashid had had some type of breakdown. His mental state was worse than I had ever feared.

Dr. Lee walked out into the waiting room and called to me. "Mrs. Ahmed."

"Yes, I'm here," I said, standing up and walking toward him.

"Please, sit down and we can talk about your husband's condition," he said as he took a chair close to mine as I sat back down. He looked at Jabeen and asked, "Is she a relative?"

"Yes, she's Rashid's sister. She's here visiting with me to help Rashid," I explained as I glanced over at her.

"So, what your husband has is a mental condition called paranoid schizophrenia. He is seeing and hearing things that aren't there. And he believes people are trying to hurt him. He's extremely delusional." Dr. Lee paused and looked me in the eye. "Can you tell me who Shelly and Anita are?"

"Yes, Shelly is his first wife and Anita is his daughter. Has he said something about them?" I was very curious what Rashid had been telling Dr. Lee concerning Shelly and Anita.

"Yes, and no," Dr. Lee answered. "Rashid believes that when the television is on, there is nothing but pictures of them. When he picks up a newspaper, he sees nothing but images of Shelly and Anita.

I was shocked. I didn't know what to say. Was Rashid so guilt ridden that he was conjuring them up in his mind on a continual basis? I asked Dr. Lee about the cause of his mental illness. "What caused him to develop this disease?" I said as I wiped a stray tear from my cheek.

"Schizophrenia is considered a hereditary disease. But it's believed severe stress can contribute to the development of it. It has been noted that stressful experiences often precede the emergence of schizophrenia."

I twisted the wedding band on my finger and stared out the window. I imagined it must have been a stressful experience to have his father order him to divorce his first wife. At that point, I started blaming Chacha Laeeq for Rashid's illness. Then turning to face Dr. Lee, I asked, "Will he ever be cured?"

"No. It's not a curable illness, but with medication he can live a somewhat normal life and function well in society. He's an intelligent man and if we can control his hallucinations, he can still offer a lot to humanity," Dr. Lee said as he stood up to leave. He had a sympathetic look on his face.

I looked at Jabeen and she had tears running down her cheeks. I gave her a hug and then led her back into Rashid's room. When we walked in, Rashid seemed to be more alert and noticed us as though for the first time. He reached for Jabeen's hand and smiled. "My sister, I'm glad you're here," he said to her. Her presence seemed to make him feel a little more secure.

Shortly after Rashid was hospitalized, he began to say that the Jews were going to try to kill him. I suppose that was because he'd worked at a Jewish medical center in Brooklyn, NY. He knew many Jewish doctors there.

One day when I visited him, he had a lit cigarette and was burning a small circle out of his pajama leg. "What are you doing?" I asked him in utter amazement. "Where did you get that cigarette?"

"Someone gave it to me. I needed to make a yarmulke." Rashid looked at me with a satisfied look on his face while he placed the small circle of cloth on his head. "Now the Jews will think I'm one of them and leave me alone."

Worried about him burning his pajamas, I asked a friend to accompany me and we walked to a synagogue. There I asked if they had any yarmulkes and, when they told me they did, I asked for one for my husband. "Here is one he might like," the lady said as she handed it to me.

I took it and went straight back to the hospital. Handing it to Rashid, I said, "Here's a yarmulke for you to wear. Keep it with you." I sat down beside his bed.

Fingering it lightly, he smiled as he looked at me. Hiding it under his pillow, he said, "Thanks, Ambreen, I'll wear it when necessary. It should be safe here." He patted his pillow. I felt glad that it made him feel safe in the hospital. I didn't like it when he felt persecuted.

Several times when visiting him, I noticed he was wearing it. Occasionally, he'd take it off when I was there, but would put it back on when his doctor came into the room.

I discovered one day, when I was visiting him, that Rashid was being devious about taking his medication, also. Wondering why he wasn't getting any better, I made the disturbing discovery that he had taken up chewing bubble gum, and when they gave him his medication, he would put it inside the gum and throw it away. No wonder he wasn't getting any better, I thought. I was almost at my wits end.

Jabeen had already gone back to her home in Calgary, and I was dealing with all the turmoil by myself. I was becoming stronger and wiser, but I still felt so alone. I had never told my parents anything about my situation in America. I didn't want to burden them with my problems, but I also didn't want them to think I'd caused Rashid's illness.

My daily trips to the hospital were wearing me down. Being pregnant took its toll on my stamina. Nevertheless, I trudged there every day; sometimes in the morning, other times in the afternoon. I was beginning to also worry about how we would live with no income during his hospitalization, because I didn't know how much we had in savings at the time. I'd already cut out buying much of anything other than a small amount of food to eat.

Dr. Lee met me coming out of Rashid's room one day and said to me, "Ambreen, I think Rashid will be more comfortable if you take him back to his own country. He'll be around his own people and will feel safer."

"Perhaps you're right," I said, thinking that I would have support from my family there in Pakistan and would be able to deal better with his illness. "I think I'll make plans to take him home right away. Thank you, Dr. Lee," I said as my hope began to grow that being around family would help cure him or, at least, make him better.

I went back to our apartment and began packing up our personal items to take to Pakistan with us. I took special care with his diplomas. He would need them when he started practicing medicine once again.

I called the airlines and booked our flight back to Pakistan. Then I went to pick him up at the hospital and take him to our apartment to prepare for our return home.

"You're taking me away from here?" he asked in a curious tone when he saw I had been packing up all our belongings. "If we're going back to Pakistan, no one from here can hurt me, right?"

"Right," I said. "You'll be better there and will be able to heal. Our family will help protect you from any harm, Rashid." I felt sure that his mental state would return to normal once we arrived back in Pakistan. If only I could keep him from getting rid of his medication.

CHAPTER TEN

I called and told my parents we were coming home. "We're happy to have you and Rashid come back. You can stay with us, if you like. Whatever you need, we'll be here for you," my abba said over the phone.

"Thank you, Abba," I said. "I'm making the plans now, so it shouldn't be too long until we're there. I'll see you and Ammi soon." I hung up the phone, and with a hopeful heart, looked at our airline tickets lying beside my purse.

Getting all our important papers together, I looked around the apartment and decided to leave everything, except our personal items. We'd be traveling light on the trip home.

It was a hot day in August of 1971 when we left for Pakistan. I was so excited I could hardly contain the exhilaration I felt. Holding Rashid's hand like a child's, we walked onto the plane and took our seats.

After the plane took off, I watched Rashid as he glanced around the plane at all the people. I was so afraid he'd start acting weird that I decided to carry on a continual conversation with him. Mostly it was about nothing important, just where we would be landing and what we might see. I was happy to see that he kept dozing off when I stopped talking.

I'd made sure he'd taken his medication by putting it in his food that morning before we'd left for the airport. I'd been doing that a lot lately, so he wouldn't be tempted to throw it out. If I had to live with him, I had to make sure he took his medicine.

I monitored his behavior all the way home. For the most part, he seemed normal, but then he'd slept a great deal. The only time I wondered if there would be a problem was when we changed planes in London.

"Oh, we're moving here," Rashid said, with a glowing smile on his face. "I've always liked London. They have good Indian food here."

"No, Rashid," I said as I gripped his hand tighter. "We're only changing planes here. We're on our way home to Pakistan."

"Okay." He lowered his head and followed me to the gate for our next flight. Sitting there at the gate waiting to board the plane, I looked at him often and saw he was looking at all the people with a suspicious look on his face.

Finally, they called for boarding and I stood up. I took Rashid's hand while he stood and then, after showing our tickets, led him down the ramp to the plane.

Being pregnant, I felt somewhat uncomfortable with the seat belt on, so periodically I would take it off when I thought it was safe to do so. I was counting down the hours until we landed in our home country, far away from Shelly.

My parents came to the airport to meet us. Ammi hugged me fiercely and I thought she'd never let go. I was pleased that she was happy to see me again. She talked all the way to the house. "Tell me all about your time in America," she said, glancing first at me and then at Rashid.

"It was nice, Ammi, but very different from here," I said. I would tell them soon all about my trials there, but I wanted to wait until Rashid wasn't sitting by my side.

Rashid and I moved into one of the bedrooms in their house and shortly after that I told the whole story to my ammi. She in turn told my abba who said to me after hearing about it, "It's okay. Go sleep and rest now. You're home."

Soon Rashid was behaving normal, or so it seemed to me. He began looking for a job. As luck would have it, there was an opening for a doctor at the construction site of the Tarbela Dam located on the Indus River in Pakistan. They offered him the job with good pay.

We moved to the area right away, so he could begin work. We were given a house to live in while Rashid was employed there. I spent much time and energy fixing it up nicely. I was growing larger as the months went by, but stayed active working on our house while counting the days until the birth of our child.

Construction of the Tarbela Dam was undertaken by an Italian firm, but there were many Americans, British and Germans working there. It seemed much like an American community. Everything appeared much like it had in the USA, so Rashid felt comfortable there, since he'd lived in America for so long after his early education.

"The Tarbela Dam Hospital is just like the hospitals in America," Rashid announced to me one day when he returned from work. "I really like it there."

"That's good to know," I said as I continued hanging new curtains in our bedroom. "I'm glad you like it, Rashid."

Rashid seemed happy since he'd started working as a doctor again. He would come home excited and tell me about some disease he'd diagnosed and I knew he was doing well. I kept track of his medicine and made sure he took it, even if I had to slip it into his food.

Most of the time, I took pleasure in watching the building of the dam. It kept me entertained and kept my mind occupied on things other than Rashid's illness and my bulging waistline.

Tarbela Dam would become the largest earth-filled dam in the world and was 485 feet high above the Indus riverbed. It forms the Tarbela Reservoir and was designed to store water from the Indus River during the monsoon period. Its supply would be for irrigation. Another important aspect of the dam was for the generation of hydroelectric power. It also was to help with flood control.

Unfortunately, there was war in 1971 when West Pakistan, my region, began a military crackdown on the Eastern part of the nation to suppress Bengali struggle for independence. Some members of the Pakistani military and supporting Islamist militias from Jamaat-e-Islami killed about 300,000 to 500,000 people and raped between 200,000 and 400,000 Bangladeshi women in a campaign of genocidal rape. The academic consensus says those were the events during the Bangladesh Liberation War.

In December of that year, I gave birth to our first daughter, Saba. Because of the war, there was a blackout when I went to the hospital to give birth. I was somewhat frightened, but excited as well. It was still dark in the hospital when she entered the world.

Saba was a tiny, dark haired baby and I fell in love with her immediately as she opened her big eyes and peered at me. I counted all her fingers and toes and examined every part of her body as soon as it was light enough to see.

"Look, Rashid, she's perfect," I said, beaming.

"Yes, she is." Rashid glanced at us and then turned away to go out of the room for some reason I didn't know.

After we got home from the hospital, Rashid seemed to be a proud father and took good care of her. When she cried, he often rushed to pick her up. I was happy to see him participating in her care. My jealousy over his other wife and daughter took a back seat at that time. I was in my home country with my family nearby and thoughts of Rashid's former life became diminished.

Soon, however, traces of his paranoid schizophrenia began to surface again. The first incidence was when we'd hired a painter to come to our house and do some painting for us. When the man arrived, Rashid called me aside and said, "I think he's a spy. He's going to tell the USA what's happening in my house." He had a look of utter terror on his face and he was shaking all over.

"It'll be okay, Rashid. I'll make sure they don't find out anything of interest here in the house," I said, looking into his eyes. I took his hand in mine and squeezed his fingers.

"Thanks, Ambreen," he said as a look of peace came over his face. He was nodding his head slowly as he glanced back at the painter.

Rashid starting taking me to the movies or dancing whenever we decided to go out for a while. We had a young babysitter whom we trusted and didn't worry about Saba when we went out. For the most part, he seemed content with our lives there in Pakistan. The past began to fade from my mind, and I felt like any other ordinary wife.

Life seemed good, and our relationship flourished for a time. Although, on a couple of occasions Rashid went into Saba's room and locked the door. "Rashid, why did you lock the door?" I asked when I tried to open it. Saba was beginning to get restless in my arms, and I'd wanted to put her in her crib.

"I'm in here reading my medical journals," he replied.

"You can read them out here if you want," I said, questioning why he needed to be locked away from me. What was he really hiding? I wondered.

"No, I'd rather read them in here." I could hear him getting up and checking the door to make sure it was securely locked.

A few years passed by before another incident with his illness occurred. Two men came to do some repairs on our house. When

Rashid saw the hammers and nails, he grew quiet and moved away from them. "They're going to hammer those nails into my skull," he whispered as he tried to stand behind me.

"Just stay close to me and it won't happen," I calmly said.

I didn't know how else to console him from his delusion then, so I said nothing more. I just patted his hand and stayed between him and the workers. I led him into another room and kept him away from the workmen until they had finished their job and left our house. Rashid calmed down totally as soon as they left.

Life became more or less routine for us. He was going to work in the Tarbela Dam construction community, and I was staying home taking care of our daughter, Saba, who seemed to grow so quickly.

I had just finished washing the dinner dishes when the phone rang. Picking up the receiver, I heard Abba's voice. "I have some bad news to tell you, Ambreen," he said. Before he could say another word, my heart leaped in my chest and I felt faint. Was Ammi ill? I wondered.

"We've just received word that your sister, Salima and her husband, Mahmood, has been in a serious car accident. They were on their way to a wedding when their car was hit head-on. Mahmood, his sister and cousin were killed instantly. Salima was thrown from the car and suffered both a head and spinal cord injury, but at least she survived." I could hear the anguish in my abba's voice.

"Oh, Abba, I'm so sorry to hear that. I'll go home to help Ammi right away," I said as tears stung my eyes.

I relayed the news to Rashid and said I'd take Saba with me. With a heavy heart, I rushed to Lahore to visit with my family.

When I arrived there, I saw that Abba was beside himself as he hovered over his favorite child. She was completely dependent upon others for her daily care. Hanging onto life precariously, it was uncertain if she would survive at all. With diminished mental capacity, her children could no longer depend on her for motherly care, so my parents took over total care of both Salima and her children.

"Ammi," I said, "are you going to be able to take care of Salima and her kids, too?" I was afraid it would be too much on my ammi and she would end up suffering.

"Of course, Ambreen. I still have Abbiee to help for a while. She's older now, but still able to help out," Ammi said as a tear escaped and rolled down her cheek.

I stayed with my parents for a short while to help, but felt I should take Saba and get back to Rashid. I packed up and left with a gloomy heart. For the first time in my life, I felt sorry for my sister, Salima and regretted that she had to suffer such a horrific accident.

In early 1975, I discovered I was pregnant again. Saba was three years old and didn't require as much of my attention as she had as a baby. I was excited to have another child and wondered if it would be a girl. I hoped it would be, and it seemed quite possible, since Rashid was the father of only daughters, so far.

In the fall of that year, our second daughter, Hanna, was born. Tiny with large dark eyes and black hair, she won my heart just like Saba had when she was born. From then on, all my time and energy was spent taking care of her and Saba. I was teaching Saba new things almost every day, it seemed. I didn't have time to dwell on Rashid's illness, and at the time, he wasn't exhibiting many symptoms.

Living with a man who is paranoid schizophrenic can make one paranoid as well, I thought as I tried to pry open Rashid's locked desk drawer in his home office. I was just sure I would find letters from both Shelly and Anita, if I could only get it open. I calculated and figured Anita must be about eight years old by then and might want to write to her father. I wondered if I'd also find pictures of them. I desperately wanted to know what Shelly looked like.

Hanna started crying, and I was pulled away from my task of attempting to open the drawer. It would have to wait, I thought, but then I never did get it open. And I never learned what he kept in that drawer.

A year later in 1976, the Tarbela Dam was completed. Rashid stayed on in the town as the internal medicine specialist. One of his diabetic patients highly praised him to the whole town. Many other people would tell me how much they liked Dr. Rashid Ahmed and how he'd cured them of some disease or got them started on the right medication. I was pleased to know he was doing well in his career.

"It seems you've made a good name for yourself, Rashid," I said to him one day when he walked through the door from work. "I've heard rumors of your excellent care for your patients."

Rashid beamed as he walked toward the dining room table and sat down to eat dinner. "I'm glad people here like me. I do the best I can to take care of my patients," he said as he snatched a chicken leg from the platter and put it on his plate.

The next couple of years, the girls were growing rapidly, and I was so busy with them I hardly had time to dwell on Rashid's illness or his symptoms which would occasionally crop up.

Late in November, 1978, I walked into Rashid's office and saw him bent over a tablet of paper. Startled when he saw me, he put his hand over the paper and said, "I'm busy right now. Please wait." His face was beet red, and his dark eyes were glaring at me. He'd been writing something that he didn't want me to see.

I didn't know what to say to him, so I said nothing. I walked away and wondered why he always had to be so secretive about his affairs. Maybe that's what it was, I thought, an affair. But no, he never seemed to be away long enough to be having an affair with another woman. Shelly was the one potential person who he may likely want to renew a relationship with, but she was in America, as far as I knew. Still, she was heavy on my mind. Maybe it's her that he's staying in touch with. He does have a child with her. But if that was the case, why didn't he just tell me he wanted to know how his daughter, Anita, was doing. Surely, he would know I'd understand his desire to be in touch with Anita.

A month later, I went to the hospital to see Rashid. The girls were home with their baby sitter. When Rashid saw me, he motioned me into his office. "Wait in here for me. I have to see a patient right now. I'll be back soon," he said and then turned and walked out the door, pulling it closed behind him.

I sat down behind his desk and looked at everything on top of it. Suddenly, I had the urge to open one of the drawers. Surprised, I saw a picture of Anita along with a letter that she had written to her father. I had to admit she was a pretty little girl, much like my own daughters. From the date on the letter, it had been written very recently. I surmised that she was about twelve then.

Eager to know what she had to say to Rashid, I quickly began reading it. I had only read a couple of paragraphs when I heard him walking close to the office. Quickly, I shoved the letter and picture back in the drawer and shut it. I looked up as Rashid entered the office.

"Are you ready to go?" he asked as he slipped his stethoscope from around his neck and dropped it on the desk. He took off his lab coat and hung it on a hook by the door.

"Yes." I stood up and walked toward him as I wondered if I'd ever get to finish reading the letter from Anita.

CHAPTER ELEVEN

Z. A. Bhutto had been elected President of Pakistan in 1970 while we were in the United States. He was one of the country's most enigmatic, flamboyant and contradictory politicians ever. There were lots of various ideologies of the left and the right, and they were fought over during the 1970's in Pakistan as well as elsewhere in the world.

In January 1974, Bhutto nationalized all banks in Pakistan as well as the many mills throughout the country. The process was not as successful as he'd hoped and, consequently, it caused a colossal loss, not only to the national treasury, but also to the Pakistani people.

Believing that there should be unity between Islamic countries, he developed closer ties with Saudi Arabia and Indonesia. Bhutto had been the country's first civilian chief martial law administrator. He was also the first civilian president.

His government of martial law had also begun the process of Islamization of Pakistan. The study of Islam in Pakistan became a compulsory subject in the schools. The religious faction, an

Islamic version of Mao Zedong's Cultural Revolution, was at work in Pakistan during that time as well.

In 1977, following civil disorder, Zia-ul-Haq deposed Bhutto in a military coup. He immediately declared martial law and had Bhutto executed less than two years later after the controversial trial by Pakistan's Supreme Court.

The primary policy of his government was the 'Sharization' of the country. Bhutto had already banned selling and drinking wine by Muslims, but Zia went further by enforcing sharia law.

With Zia at the helm, women were ordered to cover their heads while in public. Women's participation in sports and the performing arts was severely restricted, making me glad my college education was already finished.

During the 1970's, a deep suspicion of foreign powers and minority faiths began to set into the mindset of many Pakistanis. Since my family belonged to the Islamic sect, Ahmadiyya, we became the persecuted minority. The members of our sect are all highly educated people and do not believe in jihad as the rest of the Islamic culture does.

Therefore, other Muslims say we are not Muslims at all, but consider us as infidels. The leader of our sect, who is like the Pope in Catholicism, moved out of Pakistan and began telling the rest of us that we should leave as well.

One day, a young girl was burned in a chemistry department at school simply because she was a member of the Ahmadiyyas. It became clear that it was time to leave Pakistan again, perhaps for the last time.

Many in my family had already started to move to other countries. Some went to the USA, while others ended up in Canada, England, or Australia. Almost all of my aunts, uncles, cousins and brothers left. Very few remained in Pakistan.

Of course, Rashid's parents, Chacha Laeeq and Chachi Sheeba, remained there because they were very religious and couldn't stand the thought of living elsewhere.

We had started receiving threatening letters from Islamists concerning our non-compliance with Jihad. They wrote that we were not Muslims and shouldn't be living there.

Soon after, we left the Indus River valley area and moved to Karachi to live with Rashid's parents in March, 1979. I thought I'd be happy in Karachi, since it was the most cosmopolitan city; free from provincial or national prejudices. Therefore, I thought we'd be safe from harassments. Situated on the coast of the Arabian Sea, Karachi is the industrial and financial center. It is also the most secular and socially liberal cities in Pakistan. Throughout the 1960s and 1970s, Karachi was known as the "City of Lights" because of its vibrant nightlife. I was excited to move there and hoped Rashid would take me dancing frequently.

Once we moved there, I saw that living with Rashid's parents wasn't going to be easy. I rarely saw my father-in-law, for he was seldom at home. After work, he would go directly to the mosque for several hours. However, it was a test of my patience to live with my mother-in-law who was always complaining about Saba and Hanna messing up the house. "Tell them to stop jumping all the time," she said when I walked into the living room where the girls were playing.

"Yes, Chachi Sheeba," I said as I gathered the girls to my side and ushered them out of the room. I was beginning to think she didn't like me, even though I was her niece.

When Rashid asked me what was wrong, I told him, "You mother is so critical of our daughters. She doesn't want them playing in the house, nor does she want them drinking the milk. I don't know how to please her. Maybe we should put the girls in a boarding school."

"If you think that's best; okay, we will," Rashid said as he turned and walked toward the kitchen.

I found that my in-laws and I had differing beliefs about many things, making it even more difficult for me to live with them. I made arrangements for our daughters to live in a boarding school, even though the youngest girl was only three and a half. So, I packed them up and took them to the place several hours away from Karachi, but close to where my parents lived. I could visit them at the same time I visited my home. I felt I was doing the best for my daughters at the time, even though I missed them terribly. Deep down, I felt they were safe there.

One day after listening to the news, I took Rashid aside, away from his parents and said, "You know it's getting worse here for our people; those of our Ahmadiyya sect. Shouldn't we leave here like so many of our relatives have?" I watched his face closely as the idea sunk into his mind, and he slowly began to smile.

Rashid agreed with me that we should go somewhere else. "Let's go back to Canada," he said. "We won't go back to Ottawa, though. I'll see where I might be able to get a job and then we can go there." Rashid walked out of the room. I hoped he wasn't going to tell his parents that it was my idea to leave Pakistan.

Rashid made the arrangements, and honestly, it sometimes amazed me that he could function so well in certain circumstances and would appear to be totally normal mentally. "We are going to a territory in northern Canada, to a small town. Most of the inhabitants are Native Americans, which Americans call Indians." He laughed at that and then continued talking. "Most of the doctors there are British."

"I'm glad you found a place for us to live, Rashid," I said as I sat down on the sofa and wondered how soon I could bring the girls back, so we could leave. I began to make a mental list of all we would take with us. I wanted to travel light, so we'd have to have enough money to buy what we needed once we got there.

I was surprised that Rashid's parents seemed pleased we were going to America again. After our plans were made, we collected Saba and Hanna from the boarding school and packed everything we were going to take with us to Canada.

The day we left Pakistan was bright and sunny. It was early in March, 1980. I was so very happy to leave Pakistan, I felt like I was walking on clouds as I moved about packing our last-minute items to take on the plane with us.

I'd become frightened of the Islamic extremists and would be glad to put a lot of mileage between us. I'm sure we looked like a typical happy family as we boarded the plane and took our seats. I prayed that Rashid wouldn't have any symptoms of his illness anymore. He was taking his medication routinely at that time, and he looked perfectly normal.

The small town in Northern Canada was a quaint little place. Everyone seemed to be very nice. My biggest complaint was that it snowed year-round. Even in July and August there was snowfall and it was bitterly cold all the time. After one year, I sensed that Rashid was beginning to be scared of the people there, and so I asked him if we could move to another town.

"Let's go to Grand Falls in Newfoundland," he said after giving it some thought. "I've heard it's a nice place with friendly people."

"It's got to be warmer there than it is here," I said as I happily anticipated moving there. So once again, we packed up and moved. Symptoms of Rashid's illness kept cropping up, and when they did, he would feel persecuted and want to move. He'd walk out on his job without a thought. We were beginning to struggle financially again. There never seemed to be enough money to live comfortably.

After staying in Grand Falls, Newfoundland for several months, Rashid started behaving weird once again. He wouldn't eat anything I cooked. Afraid that I would poison his food, he would boil eggs to eat. When I questioned him about it, he said, "Nobody can put poison inside the egg shell without breaking it."

He had managed to obtain a partnership in a medical office with another Pakistani doctor in Nova Scotia, so we moved from Newfoundland after only being there six months.

"I've found the right doctor to practice medicine with now," Rashid said after we'd been in Nova Scotia for one month. "He isn't trying to do anything against me."

"I'm glad," I said, thinking how tired I was getting of this type of life with a mentally ill man. But at the moment he was able to function normally, and so I put up with it for the sake of our daughters.

We'd been there for a couple of months, and I was feeling secure that all would be well. No major incidents had occurred, and life was just very mundane. Rashid was off work on Wednesdays, and he decided to go to the library.

"I'm going out to the library, Ambreen," he said as he pulled his coat on and headed for the door. "I want to borrow a bible."

I turned and looked at him with an expression of disbelief. "Why do you want to borrow a bible," I asked. "Why don't you just read your Quran?"

"I want to study about Christianity," he said, giving me a haughty look of contempt. "I need to tell my enemies I am also reading the bible."

"Okay," I said as I watched him walk out the door. What harm can come of him going to the library to borrow a bible. If it will make him feel better, then it's a good thing, I thought.

About an hour later, the telephone rang and it was an employee of the library calling me. When I answered the phone, the person said, "Is this Mrs. Ahmed?"

"Yes, it is," I replied.

"Your husband is here standing on a table with a bible in his hands. He's not feeling well and we can't get him down off the table. Please come get him."

"I'll be right there," I said before hanging up.

I got the girls ready to go out and snatched my coat from the hall closet. Slipping it on, I opened the front door and ushered the girls out. We rushed to the library where I found Rashid was still on a table, jabbering away.

I finally managed to get him down and out of the library. He was shuffling his feet as we walked along. "Where are you taking me?" he asked. "To get me killed?" A hateful expression crossed his face. Did he really think I was his enemy too?

"No, I'm not going to kill you. In fact, no one is going to kill you," I answered as we got into the car.

Saba and Hanna tried talking to him and by the time we got back to the house, he had calmed down. "I'm going to cook chicken curry for dinner tonight," I said. "Just watch the girls and make sure they stay out of trouble."

"Okay." He sat staring at the girls until I left to go into the kitchen. I could hear him asking Saba and Hanna questions about me.

As we ate dinner, he seemed to be doing better. He picked at the food, shoving it around on his plate. Eventually, he started eating and seemed to enjoy it. He obviously didn't think I was trying to poison him anymore.

I checked to see if he was taking his medication, but I couldn't tell because the bottle was nearly empty. I'd have to keep track of it again, I thought to myself as I spooned some curry onto my plate.

Every day I was waking up and wondering what was going to happen with him. It became a guessing game; never knowing if he would exhibit symptoms of his illness or not.

One morning, Saba was in the living room playing with her dolls while I was busy cleaning. Hanna was down for a nap. The telephone rang and I answered it. "Hello," I said.

"Is Rashid there? He hasn't shown up for work and we're very busy," the man on the other end of the line said.

"Yes, I believe he's here," I said. "Let me find him." I put the receiver down and walked into another room. Rashid was sitting there reading a medical journal. "You're needed at work. Why are you still here?"

"Tell them I'm not home," Rashid said as he stood up and walked away from me.

I went back to the phone and said, "I'm not sure where he is right now, but I'll tell him to get to work right away."

"Thanks, Mrs. Ahmed," the man said before he hung up.

I walked through the house and couldn't find Rashid anywhere. I thought perhaps he'd gone outside. "Saba, where's your father?" I asked as she stood up and pointed to the ceiling.

"Why are you pointing up at the ceiling?" I asked with a frown on my face. I couldn't understand why Saba would point at the ceiling when I asked where her father was.

"He's up there," Saba said.

I thought she must be mistaken. How could Rashid have gone up into the ceiling? "Rashid," I called to him. "Where are you? Please tell me."

I heard a muffled noise from the ceiling and sure enough, Rashid was in the attic crawl space. There was no ladder close by and no stairs went up into it.

It took a lot of persuasion to get Rashid down out of the ceiling crawl space. "Those people are coming here to kill me," he lamented more than once. No matter what I said, he just kept repeating it over and over. He was certain that someone was going to kill him.

Finally, I convinced him that only the girls and I were in the house, and it was safe to come down. He was trembling all over when he came out of the ceiling space. I made him a cup of tea and put him on the couch with a pillow. He began to relax and started talking to me.

"I can't work with that doctor anymore. He's out to get me," Rashid uttered in a voice so low I could hardly hear. "I think we need to leave this place."

"I'm so tired of moving, Rashid. Can't you find another job here so we don't have to move again," I said as feelings of resentment began to settle over me. I was tired of constantly moving, but I didn't want him to feel like he was being persecuted.

At the time, his illness seemed to be getting worse again. I was out of my mind with worry. I called my brother, Adnan and one of Rashid's younger brothers to come to Nova Scotia. When they arrived, they were surprised at how sick Rashid really was. They stayed and helped me with him for a short while before they had to leave.

CHAPTER TWELVE

In early spring of 1981, it appeared that Rashid's illness was progressively getting worse. I was utterly distraught, so I called my cousin, Leema, who was married to one of Rashid's younger brothers. I didn't know what I should do and needed advice.

"Rashid's illness is so bad I can't deal with it. He always wants to move from one country to another or from one city to another. He's talking now about possibly going back to Pakistan. It's making me crazy, too," I said when Leema picked up the phone. "We can't have a normal life like this."

"Why have you become his puppy dog? Wherever he goes, you think you need to go, too. You should not go back to Pakistan. Why don't you come to Alberta and live with us? We can make a room for you, Rashid and your daughters in our basement," she said after listening to my story.

"I'm sure it will help Rashid to be around his brother. I'll tell him we need to move there," I said, feeling a sense of relief. It would be good to have a family member close by to talk to when things were tough.

"You can make an apartment in our basement," Leema said. "It shouldn't cost you too much to convert it. I know a good handyman who does great work on those types of projects."

"Okay, set it up with him and then tell me the cost," I said, feeling an excitement, I hadn't known for quite some time. We'd be going to a new place, and maybe Rashid's illness would subside around our relatives.

I paid the handyman $4000 to build an apartment in the basement of Leema's house. It had two bedrooms, bathroom, kitchen and living room. It was small, but would be adequate.

I packed up our belongings, oversaw the loading of the truck and drove behind it all the way to Calgary in the Canadian province of Alberta. Saba and Hanna entertained themselves by playing games such as keeping count of the different types of cars we passed. Other times, they read or played card games. I was so happy to know they could amuse themselves on the long drive across Canada.

Situated in an area of foothills and prairie, Calgary is roughly 50 miles east of the front ranges of the Canadian Rockies. "This will be our home for the next year, or more," I said as we followed Leema and Rashid's brother, Waleed, into our basement apartment. I hoped we could live there for a very long time. It would also be good for the girls to be around our relatives.

"It seems so small," Saba said, carrying in her suitcase.

"It isn't that small," I replied, looking around and thinking it really was small after all. "We'll be fine here." I noticed Rashid staring at the room before going into the bathroom. I wished his brother, Waleed would take him off my hands until we got settled.

Granting my unspoken wish, Waleed asked Rashid if he wanted to go outside with him and look around. It gave me time to try to get settled. Leema offered to cook dinner for us that night until I got things unpacked. "I'll see you all soon," she said as she left to go prepare dinner.

Later, as we sat around their dining table eating dinner, I was happy we had come to Calgary. Rashid and our daughters seemed to be delighted to be with our relatives. The girls had a cousin to play with, and that helped me to think all would be well there.

After the first several weeks, while we tried to establish ourselves in Calgary, all I could do was cry when no one was around. I continually asked God why my life had turned out like it had, and then I'd cry some more. Nothing seemed to get my mind off the terrible quandary in which I found myself. Why had I been dealt such a horrible hand?

Finally, I began to see that Leema's life wasn't perfect either, and the more I empathized with her, the less I dwelt on my own situation. I cried less and less as time went by.

Leema found a job for me in a clothing factory where she worked. It was the first job I'd ever had and was pleased I was able to do it. I truly enjoyed working with Leema, since we were on the same assembly line next to each other. We discovered that we enjoyed working together. Our job was to glue labels on the clothes. It was easy and fun. The pay was decent also; we made around ten dollars an hour. I was happy to be doing something useful besides following Rashid half way around the world and back multiple times.

I had a nice car, so I drove us to work. Leema liked to go shopping or out for lunch sometimes when we weren't working, so I was the designated driver when we went out. Some days we would just laugh most of the day; other times we would bitterly complain about our situations and our arranged marriages.

"Arranged marriages should have been outlawed," I said as we drove downtown. "We wouldn't be in these marriages, if they had been."

Leema looked at me and smiled. "I couldn't agree with you more. I wish we'd been allowed to date and fall in love. Then we could have married someone we truly loved instead of being stuck with first cousins."

"The only good thing to come out of it, though, is our children. I am very grateful to have my girls," I said, thinking to myself how beautiful they were.

"Yes, you do have a point," Leema said. "I am also grateful for mine."

When we arrived home, Rashid and Waleed were sitting outside in lawn chairs, drinking sodas. "Can you help me carry some things in out of the car?" I asked Rashid.

He got up and walked over to the car. "I'll carry those," he said, picking up two bags from the back seat.

When we got them inside, I asked if the girls were upstairs with their cousin. "Yes, I'll go get them," Rashid said as I started pulling items out of the bags and putting them away. As I opened cabinets, I regretted moving there.

I could never feel like the basement apartment at Leema's place was really my home, even though we'd paid to convert the basement into a two-bedroom apartment. I didn't feel free to claim it as my own. I was afraid to even hang a picture on the wall.

Rashid spent most of his time with his brother and seemed happy, or at least content. There were some occasions when he'd just sit and stare out into space, and I'd wonder what was on his mind. Shelly wasn't ever far from my mind, and so I wondered if she wasn't far from his, too.

Jabeen and her family had moved to Edmonton, and since it was only a three-hour drive from Calgary, we were able to see them on occasions. It almost seemed like we were back in Pakistan with so many family members around.

On one visit to Edmonton, Rashid seemed almost completely normal at first. "He seems to be better now," Jabeen told me as we worked side by side in the kitchen preparing the evening meal.

"Yes, maybe the move has been good for him." I knew not to ever think he'd be cured though. He would seem normal when he was taking his medication on a regular basis. However, he sometimes revolted and refused to take it.

By the time our visit with Jabeen's family was over, she had a look of sympathy on her face as we climbed into the car for the drive back to Calgary.

Around Christmas of 1981, after being in Calgary for almost a year, Rashid was smiling as I came in from work and said, "I found a job in Saskatoon which is located in the province of Saskatchewan."

"Why didn't you find a job here in Calgary instead?" I asked, wondering why we always had to move. I was especially upset after spending so much money to remodel the basement of Leema's house. Now we would have to leave and move elsewhere.

"It's a great offer and I didn't want to refuse it," he said as he turned to walk out the door.

So once again, we packed our belongings and started out toward Saskatchewan. Situated in the prairies, it's known for its seemingly endless fields of wheat along with its 100,000 lakes. We would be living in the city of Saskatoon. It's known as the City of Bridges, because of the great number of bridges that cross the Saskatchewan River which divides the city.

When we arrived there, we rented a very nice house, and then went out to buy furniture for it. We bought a water bed for Saba and she was thrilled. I spent much time decorating the house and felt like I'd probably live there for a long time. A feeling of peace had settled over me.

Once again, I had high hopes that all would go well with him in this new place. Rashid joined a medical office with three other doctors; one was an older man who happened to be Jewish and he was very kind. He would call frequently to inquire how the family was doing and if we needed anything. I wondered if he knew of

Rashid's mental illness. Most likely, he could tell something wasn't right with him.

Rashid seemed to get along very well with his partners in the office. The other male doctor was from Turkey and the female doctor was from Iran. Every day, when he came home from work, he would tell me how much he enjoyed working with the other doctors.

The hospital was next door to their office and it was very modern with the latest equipment. Rashid was doing so well there at that time, I found it incredible and thought maybe this was where he'd finally be happy and stop having episodes with his illness. I was grateful to his partners for making Rashid feel so comfortable there, so I hosted a dinner party for his partners and their wives. The female doctor was the only single person in his practice, but she came with the others to our dinner party.

"The food is wonderful," Dr. Springstein said as he wiped his mouth on a napkin. "I hope you'll invite us again." He laughed. Every guest was in agreement with his assessment of the food.

"Thanks. I'm so glad you liked it," I said as I mentally thanked Zareen for getting me starting in cooking lessons.

Saba and Hanna were happy in Saskatoon. They were enrolled in a very nice, new school that they loved.

After only six months, Rashid came home and said somebody was after him and we needed to move. Once again, my hopes were dashed. We left the house fully furnished and moved eighty-three miles away to Prince Albert.

It was still chilly in May, 1982, so I'd forgotten and left the heat on in the house when we moved out. We stayed in a small furnished place in Prince Albert, and our money was dwindling, because Rashid couldn't work then. I received a large gas bill for the house in Saskatoon, so I drove back there, paid the bill and gave the owner of the house some extra money for leaving our belongings behind. "You can have the furniture, or sell it if you don't want it. I can't take it with us," I said as I handed him the key to the house.

I loaded up the few things I wanted to take with me and escaped as quickly as possible. I drove straight to Prince Albert where we stayed for just a month until Rashid decided we needed to head east again.

After a little over a year of living in the provinces of Alberta and Saskatchewan, we packed up my car in late summer of 1982 and drove with the girls all the way to Toronto. We stayed there with family members for a couple of nights and then left for New York.

In Syracuse, New York, we stopped at Rashid's brother, Ismail's house for a short visit. His wife, Rabia, greeted us with a smile and hugs for all my family. "Welcome," she said as she ushered us into their house. Ismail joined us in the living room. He and Rashid had much to talk about, it seemed, so they took off into the family room and left Rabia and me with the children.

"Here's the guest room, Ambreen. You and Rashid can sleep in here this week, and I'll put the girls in the living room. I hope you'll be comfortable," Rabia said as she helped me put our luggage in the guest room.

After one week of visiting with Ismail and Rabia, I was feeling a little tense and out of sorts. It seemed to me that all of us were feeling somewhat stressed.

"I think we should end our visit here now," I said to Rashid as we prepared to have dinner. "I want to get to New York City soon."

"Okay," Rashid said as he walked out of the room and joined our daughters at the dining table.

As soon as I sat down, I thanked Rabia and Ismail for letting us visit for the week. "We are planning to leave in the morning," I said as I dished some curry onto my plate.

"Oh," Rabia said. "Thanks for letting us know." She glanced at Rashid and me before picking up her fork. "I'm glad you stopped to visit us."

The next morning, we got ready and then ate breakfast. As soon as we were ready to leave, we went into the guest room to get our suitcases, but they were missing. Rashid and I searched the entire room and looked in the closet to no avail.

"Rabia, do you know where our suitcases are?" I asked as I entered the kitchen where Rabia was drinking tea. "They aren't in the guest room, and Rashid and I can't find them. Do you know what happened to them?" I approached the table and sat down.

"Yes, they're already outside," she replied as she looked up at me. "I thought I'd help you and take them out for you."

When Rashid and I went outside, we found our suitcases in front of their garage where Rabia had put them. When Rashid saw the suitcases, tears sprang into his eyes, and the look on his face told me that he felt crushed. When we got in our car, Rashid started to cry. "Why?" he repeated over and over. Then he asked, "Why did she do that?"

"Don't worry, Rashid. Don't take it so personal. She told me she was helping us by putting them out there for us to put in the car," I said as I drove us out of Syracuse, New York. "Let's just go on to Zahid's house." I worried that Rashid was beginning to feel persecuted once again and wanted him to feel secure.

"Do you think that's all it was? Her trying to help us?" Rashid asked as he turned and looked me in the eyes.

"Yes, I'm sure of it." I concentrated on driving and talking to the girls who were laughing at something we passed. I glanced over at Rashid, and he seemed to be over his anxiety attack. I smiled when he looked at me, and turned my attention back to the road ahead of us.

All of my brothers had immigrated to the United States, and Zahid was living in Staten Island at the time. He had a small two-bedroom apartment, but welcomed us to stay with him. He worked as a banker in Manhattan.

By that time, Zahid had married Rashid's youngest sister, Husna, and they had three children. I wasn't sure how the arrangement would work out, since the apartment was so small, but at least they were willing to take us in.

"Welcome, Sis," Zahid said as he gathered me into his arms. His hug was so tight; I thought he'd crush me. He was a rather big man, and I was small. I extricated myself from his grasp and kissed him on the cheek.

"Thanks, Zahid," I said. "I don't know what we'd have done if you hadn't offered to let us live here with you. Rashid never seems content anywhere for very long."

"Let's get you settled in here, and then you can rest," Zahid said. "You can have this bedroom for you, Rashid and the girls. Our kids can sleep in the living room."

The girls were helping Rashid carry in some of our belongings. When they came in loaded down, I directed them into the bedroom Zahid and Husna were letting us use.

The next day we went to a furniture store and bought a hide-a-bed sofa for the living room for their children to sleep on. When it was delivered, I didn't feel so guilty for taking their kids room. Everyone seemed pleased with the arrangement, and I felt a sense of peace at last.

CHAPTER THIRTEEN

I enrolled Saba and Hanna in school in Staten Island, but I was unable to find a decent job and, of course, Rashid wasn't working. My education was completed in Pakistan, but it wasn't recognized here in the USA. I was looking through the want ads every day for something that I could do. Finally, I saw an ad for a babysitter and called the number.

Ralph was a single father whose wife had taken off and left him with their baby, a little girl named Allie. He worked as a camera man in Manhattan. After interviewing me, he said the job was mine if I wanted it. And I did want it. He offered me good pay, and I was happy to be able to earn a living, after having to struggle with Rashid only working off and on over the years.

Then in 1983, Zahid approached me and Rashid one day and said, "Why don't we buy a bigger house together? You can help with the down payment and we'll purchase a duplex type house. You and your girls can live downstairs and we'll live upstairs."

"Okay," I said as I noticed Rashid nodding his head yes. "It will be good for us to be around family, but still have our independence, too." I quit my job babysitting Allie after one year because we were moving to another area farther away.

Zahid found an ideal house for us north of Manhattan in New Rochelle. I gave him our share of the down payment, and we purchased the house. On moving day, my girls were excited that they would still be living so close to their cousins. I started scouring through the newspapers daily, looking for babysitting jobs since that's all I'd done for several years, but any job would be okay, I thought. Finally, I found an ad for a babysitter once again. It sounded promising, so I called, and they asked me to come for an interview. Maybe this move to New Rochelle would be good for us and our daughters.

Dressed nicely, I went to their house and knocked. A young woman with dark hair and brown eyes opened the door. She was dressed exquisitely in a pale blue dress and black high heels. A single strand of pearls was draped over the front of her dress. "Hello," she said. "You must be Ambreen. Come in, please." She held the door wide open for me to enter.

I stepped into the foyer and noticed the expensive furnishings immediately. "Yes, I'm Ambreen," I said, following her into the living room which was decorated in teal and white. I noticed a Monet painting on the wall. I opened my purse, pulled out my references and handed them to her.

"I'm Karla and this is my husband, Arlie," she said as Arlie entered the room. His dark hair was disheveled, and he was grinning widely. He was wearing Calvin Klein jeans and a polo shirt.

"Hi," Arlie said as he took my hand and shook it. "Please sit down so we can talk." As we took our seats around a cherry cocktail table, he continued, "As we told you on the phone, we work in the City."

When I gave him a blank stare, he said, "New York City, that is. Our children are already in school, so we'd need you to be here to get them off to school and then again when they get home."

After discussing the salary, which was more than I thought it would be, they said they'd check my references and call me. I drove home in excitement at the prospect of such a wonderful job.

A few days later, I received a call from Karla telling me I had the job. I hung up the phone and sent a prayer of thanks. I had scraped by financially for so long, I was looking forward to being able to afford a new car and pay my mortgage without worry. It wasn't until after I started working for them that I discovered they were fashion designers. She designed purses and belts, and he designed clothing.

I began working, but Rashid was still not doing anything. It was grating on my nerves. One day he walked into the kitchen while I was preparing dinner and said, "I'm thinking of going back to Canada."

All I could do was stare at him. Was he serious? Once again, he wanted to uproot his family and leave after buying the house with my brother.

I was so tired of all his moving back and forth around the world, I didn't care what he did. "Oh," I said. "And why do you want to go back there?"

"I've been looking at the possibility of going to the Thousand Islands area. There's an opening for a doctor in that place."

"Is that right? Well, I'm not going with you this time," I said as I glared at him for a long while. "I am not about to leave a good paying job that I like so that I can follow you around every time you have the urge to move."

He stared back at me with a confused look on his face. Finally, he said, "I understand. I'll go by myself."

Rashid made arrangements in1984 to move to the Thousand Islands area which straddles the US and Canadian border in the Saint Lawrence River. The Canadian islands are in Ontario province and the US islands are in New York. He would be living and working in the Canadian area.

Once he had his plans settled, I bid him farewell. "Take care of yourself, Rashid," I said. "When you want to take the girls for vacation, let me know. I'll drive and meet you half way."

"I will," he said. "As soon as they're out of school, they can come and spend the summer with me."

I knew he loved his daughters and didn't think twice about letting him take them. After all, they were older and didn't require much care. It would make Saba and Hanna happy to spend time with him.

Busy with my life and job, the time flew by and school was out for the summer. Rashid told me he wasn't able to drive half way to meet me, so I put them in my car and drove all the way to Thousand Islands area to drop them off.

"Call me when they're ready to come back home," I said as I hugged them goodbye and got in my car for the long drive back to New Rochelle.

I watched them in the rear-view mirror for a short while as I drove away. They continued waving at me. I was missing them already.

At home, I submerged myself in work. I'd always loved plants, and I began growing a small flower garden. When I wasn't babysitting, I was gardening, and I was relatively happy at that time.

With the girls gone for the summer, I spent a lot of time with Zahid and his wife, Husna. My brother's best friend, Jasim, was visiting one day when I went upstairs to see them. "Ambreen, this is my friend; actually, my best friend, Jasim," Zahid said as I entered the living room.

"Nice to meet you," I said and then walked past them into the kitchen to talk with Husna. I heard Jasim saying, "Nice to meet you, too."

"Jasim was a famous hockey player in India," Husna said as she stirred the boiling concoction on the stove. "He's a very nice man, also."

"Really?" I said, impressed at meeting someone who had been famous. "He does seem nice."

Over dinner I had a chance to talk to Jasim and was glad to make his acquaintance. I was sure we'd see more of each other over the years.

A week before school was to start; I got a phone call from Leema. She was so excited when she told me her plans. "I'm going to New York to visit. I'll be flying into Toronto and Rabia will pick me up there. She's going to drive us on to New York City."

"That's great, Leema. I'm anxious to see you," I said as I wondered if I dare ask if she and Rabia could pick up the girls from Rashid and bring them home. I took the plunge and said, "Do you think you and Rabia could pick up Saba and Hanna from Rashid and bring them home with you?"

"I'm sure it will be alright with Rabia. You know how kind she is," Leema said.

"Yes, I do," I said as I remembered our stay at their house for a week. "Let me know for certain if you and she will get them for me, so I don't have to drive up there and back."

"Okay, I will. See you soon," she said right before she hung up.

Things went as planned and Rabia picked up Leema, and they retrieved the girls from Rashid and drove them to my house. Saba was frustrated when she and Hanna got out of the car.

Later that night, after Leema and Rabia left, she confessed to me that Rashid didn't seem to exhibit any signs of mental illness while they were there and wondered if I'd consider going back to him.

"I can't do that, Saba," I said, sighing. "I've tried my best to help him, and he keeps going from one place to the next too frequently for me anymore. I'm getting too old to hop from place to place at a moment's notice."

I called Rashid that night to let him know I appreciated him letting the girls come home with Rabia and Leema. "Rashid, I hope you do well with this new job you have. And I hope it lasts for a long time," I said after thanking him.

"I think I'll work here until I retire," he said. "Tell the girls I hope to see them again soon."

I hung up the phone and went to get ready for bed. Tomorrow would be a busy day, getting school clothes and supplies for Saba and Hanna to start school again, I thought as I crawled into bed.

After school started, we'd get an occasional phone call from Rashid to see how Saba and Hanna were and, of course, he always inquired how I was doing. I let him know I was quite happy with our situation and his calls became less and less.

Rashid had been working in the Thousand Islands area of Canada for almost one year. I thought maybe he'd stay there indefinitely, but suddenly I got a call from him saying that he was going to Pakistan. "I cannot live here anymore," he said when I asked him why. "I'm going home to Pakistan where people aren't trying to kill me."

"Will you stop here and say goodbye to your daughters?" I asked. "They'll be disappointed that they won't be able to see you."

"They can come to Pakistan to see me," Rashid said.

"We'll see," I said, but was thinking 'over my dead body will they go to Pakistan to see you'. Things were getting so bad there for our sect, Ahmaddiya, that I didn't want my girls anywhere near there, even though they weren't practicing Muslims.

CHAPTER FOURTEEN

I was getting on with my life in 1985 and felt some reprieve that I didn't have to worry about Rashid anymore. Saba and Hanna were enrolled in a very good school in New Rochelle, and I was happier than I'd been in a long time. My job was wonderful, and I enjoyed the children I took care of for Arlie and Karla.

My parents surprised us when they came to the USA for a visit. I was thrilled to see them. "Ammi, I'm so glad you came. Please tell me you can stay for a long time," I said, looking at my abba.

"We'll be here almost one month," Ammi said. "We can't stay any longer though, because Farida is taking care of her mother for us." Farida was Salima's adult daughter.

Abba had a look of tenderness on his face when he looked at me and said, "It's so pitiful to see your sister in that condition where she can't do anything for herself. I'm not even sure she can think." I felt great sorrow for my parents concerning Salima.

Zahid and I were busy for the next month showing our parents the sights of New York City and its surrounding area. Ali and Adnan came with their families, and we had quite a special reunion.

"I would like to take them to Washington, D.C. to see the capital and maybe even stop in Philadelphia on the way home," I said to Zahid one day while our parents were napping.

"That's a great plan. Let's all go and show them the sights. I'd like to take my kids there again," he said as he began planning our trip.

Abba and Ammi were happy to go with us on that excursion and seemed to totally enjoy every minute of it. The time seemed to fly by, and it was time to see them off at the airport. I wiped the tears from my eyes as I watched them walk down the jet way at Kennedy International Airport to board their plane for Pakistan.

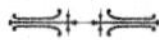

As the years started going by, I thought my life had finally taken a turn for the best. Then one day, I was busy doing laundry when the doorbell rang. I hurried to the door and there was Rashid standing on the porch. "What are you doing here now?" I questioned him. "I thought you were happily ensconced in Pakistan."

"I had to come see you and the girls," he said, a grin spreading across his face. "I've missed you, Ambreen. And I really miss Saba and Hanna."

It dawned on me that he was still standing in the doorway, so I stepped back and let him enter. "How long do you intend to stay here?" I asked.

"I'm not sure." He had walked to the sofa and sat down. "I'm thinking of moving back here or to Canada."

"Well, good for you," I said, but wasn't sure I meant it. I just knew I didn't want him interrupting my new life that I had worked so hard to make for myself and our daughters.

"I'd like to stay here for a while, so I can make plans, if that's okay with you," Rashid said, turning to face me.

"Yes, you can stay in the guest room," I said as I led him to it. "Where's your luggage?"

"It's in the yard," he said, grinning. "I wasn't sure if you wanted me here or not." He rushed outside to pick it up and brought it into the house. As soon as he'd put his things in the bedroom, the girls returned from school.

Happy to see him, they clambered around him all evening until bed time. Saba and Hanna both had smiles on their faces as they drifted off to sleep. I was glad that they seemed happy. Their lives had had as much upheaval and bewilderment as mine because of Rashid's illness. They had missed him terribly when he'd gone back to Pakistan for a while.

After a few days of staying with us, I noticed his behavior was strange once again. My friend, Mary, came to visit me and Rashid disappeared into another room. Mary and I sat in the kitchen drinking tea and talking. Suddenly, it dawned on me that I hadn't seen Rashid in quite some time.

"Excuse me, Mary, but I'm not sure where Rashid is. Let me see if I can find him so you can meet him." I walked into the living room, then the bedrooms, but didn't see him anywhere. Finally, I walked over to the hall closet and opened the door. There was Rashid, sitting on the floor of the closet. Unfortunately, Mary had gotten up from the dining table and followed me. I was so embarrassed to have her see him sitting in the closet.

"What are you doing there, Rashid?" I asked in bewilderment.

"Just resting," he answered without moving.

"Just come out of there, please," I said, turning to look at Mary who had a look of confusion on her face. I had told Mary a little about Rashid's illness, but had never told her all the embarrassing episodes which had occurred over the years.

Rashid stood up and walked out of the closet. I introduced him to Mary and as soon as I did, Mary said, "Nice to meet you." She turned to me and said, "I really need to get home, Ambreen."

I walked her to the door and said goodbye. Rashid was sitting on the couch with his head down when I walked back to the living room. He stayed for two months before he decided he needed to go back to Pakistan.

The next couple of years rolled by without any major incidents. Rashid wrote letters or called on occasions. I was thrilled to have him on the other side of the world where I wouldn't have to suffer the consequences of his illness.

Then one day in the summer of 1989, he made another appearance in New York. I was so unhappy to see him on my doorstep that I wasn't sure I wanted him to stay in my home. But then Saba and Hanna would want to be around their father, I thought as I felt I should let him stay.

He remained there like a guest for a short while. He seemed to notice how cold I'd grown toward him. He approached me one day as I sat reading a book. "Is it over between us, Ambreen?" he asked in a timid voice.

"Yes, as far as I'm concerned, it's over. In fact, why don't you marry somebody else? Maybe one day, I'll find someone else, too, and we can both start new lives. Obviously, we're not good for each other, and I'm sorry that because of me your life is ruined. But my life is ruined, also. I was deceived in the beginning into thinking you were an available husband, when in fact you were still married to Shelly. I feel like I was a sacrificial lamb in this marriage and I just can't take it anymore." I sat staring at him and noticed the look of astonishment on his face.

"I'm done following you around the world and I don't want my daughters to ever go to back to Pakistan and have the same thing happen to them that happened to me. I want them to live in this country and marry anybody they want. And as far as religion is concerned, it doesn't matter to me what religion they choose." I was on a roll letting Rashid know how I really felt.

Rashid had his head down, not looking at me. I wondered if I'd made him feel so awful that it would send him over the edge with his illness again, but I couldn't stop myself from saying, "If you'd like to, call Shelly and see if you can go back to her. If she'll have you back, maybe you'll be happy again." He looked up at me then and I thought I saw a flicker of interest. "Although, you did ruin her life as well."

I noticed a crestfallen look cross his face. He looked away and I thought I saw a tear on his cheek. I should feel ashamed for saying those things, but honestly, at that moment I couldn't feel sorry anymore.

I felt I'd done the best I could over the years, catering to a mentally ill man who had deceived me into marrying him when he already had a wife. But it wasn't just him who deceived me; it was our family who kept vital information from me and betrayed me, also.

The pain and heartache I'd endured over the years was more than any person should have to deal with. I was at the point where I just wanted a normal life. If that meant I would live as a single mom for the rest of my life, then so be it. And looking back over the years, could I even call what I'd lived through a marriage?

The next evening, Rashid came into the kitchen where I was cooking rice and cutting up vegetables. He stood close to me and said, "I called Shelly. She told me she's involved with someone else now. I didn't ask her if she'd like to get back together."

"Why not? I believe you've pined for her all these years. Now you have a chance at reconciliation with her, and you didn't ask her?"

"I didn't want to mess up whatever happiness she has in her life now," Rashid said as he picked up a small carrot and stuck it in his mouth.

I thought about it for a minute or two. I tried to look at Shelly's point of view. Perhaps she'd be afraid to welcome him back for fear he'd only leave her again, breaking her heart for a second time. "Rashid, did you really think Shelly would welcome you back after you deserted her and Anita? I know I wouldn't take someone back if they'd deserted me," I said as I continued to chop celery.

"I guess I'll go back to Pakistan then," Rashid said as he walked out of the room. "I'm going for a drive right now."

He had rented a car the previous week, because I wasn't willing to take him everywhere he wanted to go. I guess he needed to feel a little independence from me anyway.

Later that night, I searched Rashid's belongings while he was still out. I found a name with an address and phone number for a John Sinclair in West Virginia. That must be Shelly's father or brother, I thought as I copied the number down.

The next day, when Rashid was out again, I called the number I'd found. When a man answered the phone, I asked, "May I please speak to Shelly?"

"I'm sorry, but Shelly doesn't live here. She's in California and has been for many years," the man on the phone told me.

"Thank you," I said and hung up quickly. I didn't want Rashid to know I was trying to search for Shelly. For some reason, I had a desire to meet her and Anita. I had a gut feeling she'd be sympathetic to my plight. I started regretting not staying in touch with her so many years ago. Our daughters could have met and become close as sisters. I consoled myself with the fact I'd had too much to deal with over the years.

A few days later, Rashid had packed his belongings and was ready to go to the airport. I walked him out and saw him drive off in his rental car. The tears began to flow, and I wasn't sure why. Was I crying for him? For myself? For our girls? It didn't matter who the tears were for; it just felt good to release them.

CHAPTER FIFTEEN

A few months later, Zahid stopped by to talk to me. "Ambreen, I think Rashid is doing well in Pakistan now. He's been working in a hospital for leprosy patients. I talked to him last night and he seems to be happy."

"Good. I'm glad he's happy. Maybe he'll get remarried over there," I said. I picked up my cup of tea and took a sip.

"But you're not divorced yet," Zahid reminded me. "Are you seriously planning to divorce him?" I noticed he'd developed somewhat of a scowl on his face just then.

"I've thought about it for a long time and, yes, I do want a divorce," I said, looking Zahid in the eyes. "I've had a miserable life living with a mentally ill man. I'm going to ask Abba if he can draw up the divorce papers for me."

"Well, okay, but I hope it doesn't send Rashid over the edge. He's not well, you know." Zahid was looking at me like I was the crazy one.

I laughed. "If anyone in this world knows that he's not well, it's me," I said. "I'm going to tuck the girls in and get ready for bed. You can let yourself out and lock the door as you leave."

"Alright, goodnight, sis," Zahid said. "I hope you're not mad at me for reminding you about poor Rashid's illness. It's very sad for all our family; not just him." I heard the door open and close as I walked into the girls' bedroom to check on them.

At first, I didn't do anything about obtaining a legal divorce. We'd been separated off and on for several years by that time, and I saw no real rush in filing. I just let things slide by like I normally had when I'd lived with Rashid.

Finally, I thought about it more and more; especially if I ever wanted to get remarried. I wasn't sure if there would even be a possibility of that happening, but, just in case, I should get out of my marriage to Rashid.

One day in 1991, I called my abba in Pakistan and asked him if he could draw up the papers for my divorce. "Why after all these years have you now decided you need to divorce Rashid, Ambreen? Is that really what you want?" he asked after I pleaded my case.

"Abba, you know how miserable I've been for years. First, I found out I'd been deceived, and then I found out I was married to a mentally ill man. It's all become more than I can take. I want out of this marriage more than anything. He comes and goes at will and it makes me crazy, too. Please Abba, will you file it for me?" My voice was ready to break; the tears I had tried to stifle were now in the back of my throat.

"Alright, I'll start the divorce proceedings," Abba said quietly into the phone.

"Thank you so much. Now maybe I can finally have a life," I said before we hung up. Abba was coming through for me after all. Maybe he really did love me all along, but just hadn't shown it. I could only hope so.

One week later, Abba called me. "Ambreen," he said when I answered. "I have some news for you. I've drawn up the divorce papers for you, but they will need your signature. I can get Rashid's since he's here in Pakistan. So, I'm going to mail them to you. Once you sign, mail them back to me, and I'll file them with the court."

"Oh, Abba, thank you. You're a life saver," I said as I jumped with glee. "I'll mail them right back the day after I get them."

Several days later, a large envelope arrived from Pakistan for me. I eagerly opened it and pulled out the divorce papers Abba had drawn up. I scanned through them quickly, and then I sat down to read over them carefully. When I was satisfied they contained everything I wanted them to say, I picked up my pen and signed my name to the final sheet of paper.

The next morning, I drove to the post office and mailed them back to Abbottabad, Pakistan. Feeling smugly satisfied, I stopped at an Indian restaurant and ordered rice pudding. One of my favorite desserts, I seemed to crave it when I was feeling very content. And getting Rashid out of my life gave me that sentiment.

I savored the rice pudding as I sat there by myself, thinking about the past twenty years. I felt I had earned the right to a little bit of happiness in my life after all the upheaval I'd dealt with in the past. Shelly popped into my mind and I wondered how happy she was in her life. I must ask Saba and Hanna if they would like to find their half-sister, Anita, I thought as I spooned another scoop of pudding into my mouth. If they wished to meet her, maybe we could pursue finding her in California.

I paid for my pudding and left the restaurant. I drove home with a feeling of gratification at long last. By the time I reached home, I was actually euphoric and waltzed into the living room where Saba and Hanna were watching television.

"Home from school already?" I asked them, not looking at the clock.

"Mom, don't you know what time it is?" Saba asked as Hanna looked at me like I was some alien who had just landed on earth.

⁂

In early 1992, Rashid made another appearance in New York. Always surprised by his arrival back into our lives, I really didn't want him to stay in my house. Our divorce was almost final and I felt I really had nothing to say to him, much less have anything in common to do with him other than be with our girls.

However, I made the effort and starting talking to Rashid as we sat in the living room drinking tea. Saba and Hanna were out playing with their cousins, so we had all the privacy for talking about anything that we desired. There were some questions I'd not had an adequate answer to in all the years of our marriage. "Why didn't you fight for Shelly when your father ordered you to divorce her?" I asked.

"I did." Rashid was staring at me like I was the crazy one.

"What do you mean, you did?"

"I had just told my parents that I'd married Shelly and they threw a fit. My father summoned me home to Pakistan immediately. He told me if I didn't go, he'd send someone to get me and take me there." Rashid paused and looked preoccupied as though remembering the events of that time.

"Really?" I said.

"Yes, so I went to Pakistan. When I got there, I spoke to my father and begged him not to ruin my life; that I already had a wife and a child. I was crying, so he seemed ready to give in and let me lead my own life, but your father showed up just then and my fate was sealed."

"How so?"

"When my father said that I'd married someone in the United States, your father said, 'It's okay. A lot of young men have their dalliances before their real marriage."

"So, my father definitely knew about your marriage and yet went ahead and planned my marriage to you."

"Yes, he did," Rashid said.

I had always suspected that Abba knew about Rashid's marriage to Shelly, but I could never find out for certain from him. Now I knew positively, and I felt an anger toward my father arise within me. I got up and went to make dinner before Saba and Hanna came dashing in proclaiming that they were starving.

Zahid and Husna decided to host another one of their dinner parties the next night since Rashid had made his grand entrance back into our lives. Of course, they were pleased to see him again and he was always welcome in their home. However, since they had three children, they had no space for him to stay, and therefore, I was stuck with him staying in my guest room again.

When it was time to go to the dinner party, we walked upstairs and greeted everyone. Zahid's best friend, Jasim, was there as usual. As we walked in, he stood up out of respect for me as he always did when I entered a room where he was. Jasim was a very nice and respectful man. I was impressed with his behavior toward me.

It was the first time Rashid met him. He told us about why he left India and came to the USA. I felt sorry for him as I sat and listened to his tale of woe.

He'd been in love with a girl in India, but his parents arranged a marriage for her with his younger brother. Unable to tolerate being around them because of his feelings for her, he immigrated to America.

Rashid sat there listening and nodding his head the whole time. I wondered if he really was paying attention to Jasim's spiel. Shortly thereafter, dinner was served. Husna outdid herself with all the delectable dishes and everyone complimented her on the food. She was beaming with pride as she picked up a piece of naan and tore it in half.

When the party was over, Rashid and I took the girls back downstairs to my house. Saba and Hanna were so sleepy that we got them tucked into their beds as soon as they were in their pajamas and had their teeth brushed.

Rashid and I went into the living room to talk. "Jasim seems like a good man. Why don't you marry him? He's single," Rashid said, glancing at me.

I laughed at his comment. "How could I tell him to marry me?" I said, thinking that it would take a lot of audacity to do something like that. "I can't do that. Why don't you tell him?"

"How can I tell Jasim to marry my wife?"

We both laughed as we realized neither of us could say such things to Jasim.

"Our divorce will be final soon. Why don't you go back to Pakistan and marry our cousin, Ahlam? She's not married, and you might be good for her," I said. "She's living with her brother right now. Go and ask her when you get back home."

"How can I tell her I want to marry her? She's twenty-five years younger than me," Rashid said. I could tell he was seriously contemplating doing it. He'd become good about doing what he was told to do.

"When you get back to Pakistan, go to her brother's house and give her a perfume. Then tell her you'd like to marry her. Maybe she will agree." I was looking at the clock, but thinking how soon I could get him out of my hair, so I wouldn't have to worry about him anymore.

"Ambreen, you're brilliant. I would've never thought of that. Thank you for being a good wife all these years and taking care of me. Even now, although we're divorcing, you are still looking out for my welfare. Thank you from the bottom of my heart," Rashid said, taking my hand in his and looking into my eyes.

"You know I only want what's best for you, Rashid," I said as I stood up to get ready for bed. "I'm going to bed now. Goodnight."

"Goodnight," he said and got up and walked to the guest room.

Rashid stayed a couple of more days and then left for Pakistan. I knew if he married Ahlam I probably wouldn't see much of him again. I felt a mixture of both relief and sorrow as I followed him to drop off his rental car and then take him to the airport. I watched him walk into the terminal and then drove home.

Who knows what lies ahead of us, I thought as I walked back into the house. My girls were getting older and soon wouldn't need me as much. Saba was already in college at Maryland University at that time, and Hanna was in high school.

They weren't happy about the divorce, but they understood. One day, Saba came home from Maryland and we'd been up to see my brother and his family. Jasim was there. When we arrived home that night, Saba said, "Mom, Jasim's a good man. Why don't you marry him?"

"I can't just marry him, if he doesn't ask me," I said, turning to look at Saba.

"You should go out on one date to see how he is. I found out he's looking for a wife, and I told him we're looking for a husband for you, Mom," Saba said as she picked up a book to read.

Jasim and I did go out on one date. He took me to an Indian restaurant for lunch and he was so respectful of me. He was easy to talk to and seemed very attentive. I enjoyed getting to know Jasim better and hoped things would work out for us. I needed to be rescued from my family. No one was talking to me at that time, because I'd divorced Rashid.

After that, I didn't hear from Jasim for over a month. I thought perhaps he'd decided he didn't like me enough to marry me after all. Finally, I heard from him again.

"Hello," I said when I picked up the phone.

"Hi, Ambreen, I just got back home from my vacation to London and thought I'd see how you are," Jasim said. "I was there for a month visiting with relatives."

"I'm glad you're back," I said, feeling relieved that he was still interested in a relationship.

"Let's meet and talk," Jasim suggested.

"Okay. Do you want to come here to my house?"

"Fine. I'll be there in a few minutes," he said and then hung up.

I set out a platter of meats and heated up some naan. I thought we could talk over a light dinner. I boiled water for making tea.

I dashed to the door when I heard a knock. Flinging it open, I saw Jasim standing on the porch, looking fit and trim.

"Come in," I said as I held the door open for him. "I have something to eat, if you're hungry."

"Yes, I am hungry," he said as he followed me into the kitchen.

As we were eating, Jasim looked across the table at me and said, "So let's get married."

"Okay," I responded and felt myself blushing. At last I felt I was going to be rescued from my lonely life. I had no one in my family to talk to except my daughters who weren't there at the time."

"Should we tell anyone yet?" Jasim asked.

"No, not yet. Let's wait until we decide where and when we will get married." I didn't want my brothers creating a fracas for us.

From that day, we started to make plans for our marriage, but didn't set a date yet. We wanted to be sure we were doing the right thing, and waiting until we were certain seemed like the best thing to do.

I called to tell my parents. "Jasim and I are getting married. I'm not sure just when, but it should be soon," I said when my abba picked up the phone.

"That's good, Ambreen," Abba said. "Just make sure you know what you're doing this time. Your first marriage didn't work out, and I'd hate to see you so unhappy again."

Just whose fault was it that I married Rashid, I wondered while I listened to my abba on the phone. I wanted to make my own decisions from now on. If I was happy or unhappy, it would be because of my own choice.

Of course, I didn't tell Abba that. "I'm reasonably sure I'll be happy with Jasim, Abba," I said. "Saba and Hanna are growing up and I really don't want to be alone, if I don't have to be. I believe Jasim will be a good husband for me, too."

When I hung up the phone, I sat down on the sofa with a cup of tea and reminisced about my life and all I had finally accomplished. I also had a sense of fulfillment knowing I'd raised two lovely and intelligent girls who were such a delight to me.

CHAPTER SIXTEEN

I'd been babysitting for Arlie and Karla for a very long time, it seemed. Their children were growing up, just like mine were. Soon I wouldn't have a job.

I was only working for them on a part time basis then and as we sat around the kitchen counter drinking tea, Karla said, "Why don't you go to college and get a teaching degree? You already have a degree from Pakistan, so it wouldn't be hard for you to finish up here." She patted me on the hand.

"I don't know if I can afford to go back to school now at my age. My oldest daughter, Saba, is already in college, and it takes a lot of money for her tuition. Hanna will need money for college also in a few years." I liked the idea of becoming a teacher in the US, but it seemed only a dream at that moment.

"Arlie and I can help you with some of the fees, Ambreen. Over the years you've become like family to us," Karla said as she picked up her iced tea and took a sip.

So, I followed the advice of Karla and Arlie and enrolled in Hudson County Montessori School for teachers. I was excited, but scared. Could I go to college full time and still help Saba and Hanna with their educations? I wasn't sure how it would work out, but I prayed for the best to happen.

I began going to school and studied very hard. I knew I would have to do well in my studies in order to get a good job. Jasim was also going to college and working part time. Finally, we set a date and started planning the wedding. We were getting married in April, 1993.

My close friend, Abir, came to visit me. "Jasim and I are planning to marry," I told her as I set a plate of fruit on the table for us.

Abir grabbed my hands and squeezed them in excitement. "Oh, Ambreen, you must have a Muslim wedding ceremony. I will make the arrangements for you to get married at my house. I have enough room for you to invite a lot of your friends and relatives. I am so excited for you. You deserve some happiness after all you've been through," she said as she pulled out a pen and paper and began to write down all she wanted to have for my wedding.

"Thank you, Abir," I said as I started to pour tea for us. I mentally calculated how many guests I wanted to invite. I knew we'd have to have a legal ceremony also, probably at City Hall.

Our wedding day arrived and I dressed in a nice red suit with gold embroidery on it. It should have been the color of my wedding dress in Pakistan, since most brides choose that color. Jasim and I drove to Abir's house where a Muslim priest was already waiting to marry us. As soon as the ceremony was over, we began our celebration dinner.

My brother, Adnan, was the only close relative who showed up for the wedding. None of my other relatives attended because they were unhappy that I'd divorced Rashid, but I tried not to think about it and just enjoyed the day. It was a fun wedding, much unlike my first one.

Later, Jasim and I went to City Hall and got married again there, just to make sure of legalities. We didn't want to find out our marriage wasn't official after we'd been living together for a while.

One month after our Muslim wedding, we had a party at the Taj Mahal Hotel so that many of my friends and relatives could attend the celebration. The room was packed with many of my cousins in attendance. Just about everyone I knew came to the party to congratulate Jasim and me.

My parents were visiting from Pakistan, so they could celebrate my new marriage. I was so pleased that they came. I wanted them to stay permanently. However, my sister, Salima, was still in a vegetative state mentally. She would sometimes laugh or cry, but she was unable to talk or communicate her needs or thoughts to anyone.

At the party, I approached Abba and asked about her. "How's Salima doing now," I asked him.

"Your sister isn't doing well. It seems she may not live much longer," he said in a low tone. "You mother is struggling with it, too." He had a sad countenance on his face just then.

"She's been living for quite a long time already. Maybe she'll live a while longer," I said, hoping to make my abba feel better.

"Your ammi has such a burden taking care of her. It might be good for everyone if she passed. She's only a shell of her former self anyway and requires so much care." Abba glanced over at my ammi with a tender look on his face.

Ammi lowered her eyes and then said, "I hate to admit it, but I feel it would be God's blessing if he took her first instead of me. I don't know who would look after her if I wasn't able to do it. Farida has her own life now, too."

"Don't feel bad, Ammi," I said, putting my arm around her shoulder. "You have done so much over the years. You are to be praised."

She gave me a slight smile before moving over to talk to Zahid and Husna who had just walked into the room. It seemed all my brothers wanted to attend the celebration, either because they had forgiven me for the divorce or simply because they wanted to attend a party. I wasn't sure which.

My parents stayed for over a month until they had to return to their home in Pakistan. Standing at the window in the airport, I broke down and cried when their plane lifted off and soared skyward.

Saba moved back from Maryland to finish her college degree in New York. I was happy to have her live at home with me again. Jasim was pleased that she'd accepted him as a step-father. Hanna was still in high school, but would graduate soon and begin college in Canada because the tuition was cheaper there.

I was relatively happy in my new marriage. Jasim treated me and my daughters with respect and was very considerate of my feelings. No longer did I have to watch what I said or did, nor did I have to move every time my husband thought someone was going to kill him. What a relief I felt.

During a break from our college classes the following year 1994, Jasim suggested we go to India so I could see his ancestral home as well as other places. I was a little apprehensive about going because of the fighting that happened so much between India and Pakistan, but I agreed because I truly wanted to go.

The day we left, I was so excited. I would be meeting new in-laws and hoped they would like me. I also liked the prospect of seeing the Taj Mahal while in India. It was one of the places I most desired to visit.

When we landed in New Delhi, we were met at the airport by Jasim's four sisters. A lovely bouquet of flowers was thrust into my hands while all clambered around to hug me. My fears of being in an enemy country dissipated as each sister pulled me into a tight hug.

Jasim took me to the small city Rampur where his family lived. When we arrived at his grandparents' ancestral home, I felt such peace within my soul. It reminded me of my own grandparents' home in Pakistan.

The first place Jasim took me was to Agra to see the Taj Mahal. Standing in front of it at a distance, I marveled at the ivory-white marble mausoleum. Located on the south bank of the Yamuna River, it was commissioned to be built in 1632 by the Mughal emperor, Shah Jahan. It was to house the tomb of his favorite wife, Mumtaz Mahal. The tomb was the centerpiece of the complex which included a mosque and a guest house. I was amazed by the formal gardens that surrounded it on three sides.

I had to pinch myself to see if I was dreaming. To think I was actually standing in front of the famous Taj Mahal. To me, it was a dream come true, and Jasim had made sure I saw it.

When we returned to the United States, we settled back into our usual routines, and soon school began again. I put all of my energy into school work and learning all I could in order to get a good teaching job. It was certainly a struggle at times as I was already in my forties by then, but with determination, I kept plugging along and doing the best I could.

By then, Hanna had graduated from high school and had begun college in Canada. I was grateful that her tuition wasn't as much as it would have been in the USA.

My friends, Arlie and Karen, were being very supportive of me. Without their help, I don't know if I could have continued in school. Jasim was still going to college and working part time at the library in Princeton University. Our family was all studying at colleges during that time, so we were usually busy with our studies and didn't have a lot of time to spend together.

After attending the Montessori school for two years, I graduated with honors. I took the final exam and passed with flying colors even though it was a tough test. I was very pleased as I accepted my diploma.

I started looking for teaching jobs in the area and found one almost immediately. It was a job as a kindergarten teacher. I loved kids and couldn't wait to start. I made my lesson plans and, with excitement in my heart, I went to the first day of school.

I'd had low self-esteem as a child, and I wanted to instill in my students a sense of self-worth. I started praising each and every student for something they were good at, whether it was coloring, art or spelling.

There was one little dark-haired girl in my kindergarten class that reminded me of myself when I was that age. She was shy and hung back from the others. When I complimented her on something, she would lower her head and look at the floor. I must have been much like that, I thought, and I went out of my way to make her feel secure and welcomed at school.

After teaching there for a year, Jasim brought up the subject of relocating. "How do you feel about us buying a house in New Jersey," he said one evening as we were eating dinner.

"I think I might like to live in New Jersey. It's still close enough to my family that I could see them occasionally," I replied as I picked up a piece of naan and tore it in half. I took a bite of it and then continued, "I'm getting tired of being in New York anyway. And New Jersey might be a good place to live."

"Good. Let's start looking for a house close to Newark. I've heard the prices are very good there," he said as he picked up his cup of tea and took a sip.

We began looking at houses for sale and one we toured caught my eye as an ideal place to live. It was a three-bedroom, two bath house on a secluded street. There were oak trees lining the side of the road. "I'd like to have this house,' I said as I grabbed Jasim's hand.

"Okay, then we'll put an offer on it," he said, walking towards the real estate agent who was showing us the house. I watched as Jasim started talking to the gray-haired agent who was pulling out a pen from his shirt pocket, and then I stepped out onto the back patio.

I envisioned a small garden that I'd plant close to the house. I would like to grow some tomatoes as well as squash. There was a Gala apple tree next to the fence. I walked over to it, plucked an apple and bit into it. The apple tasted sweet and I was so happy we were going to buy the house.

We drove home that day thinking about all we needed to do in order to move into our new home. The day the realtor called and told us the house was ours and we could pick up the keys, we rushed to get them and made arrangements to move.

Hanna was home from college, and she helped us pack our belongings. "I've decided to go into computer work," she said as she grabbed a stack of sheets and dumped them in a box. "I really find it an interesting subject."

"If that's what you like, then you should do it," I said as I taped the box shut. "Follow your dreams in working in a field you like." I was proud of my youngest daughter and knew she'd do well in whatever she chose to do in life.

I was equally proud of my oldest child, Saba, who was working in a hospital, doing her internship for her degree in medical technology. She would be graduating soon with a BS degree.

I was surprised when she chose that profession as I had thought she might want to follow in her father's footsteps and become a physician. She explained to me that she really liked the laboratory setting where they performed examinations of human body fluids and tissues.

Finally, moving day arrived, and the movers picked up our furniture and other items and took them to our new home. I had decided to buy a few new pieces of furniture, so I needed to look for items to enhance the décor I had chosen. A new painting was ready to hang in the living room.

We worked hard getting everything organized and put in its place. When I surveyed our new home that night before bed, I smiled and a sense of gratification overcame me.

Jasim was already in bed. He'd worked hard moving furniture where I decided I wanted it. I knew he was exhausted, and I didn't want to disturb him, so I went into the guest room and crawled into bed.

I was very happy in our new house, but it was a long drive to the school where I worked. I started putting in applications and soon found a teaching job close to where we lived. I had to get used to working with different people, but it wasn't as difficult as I'd imagined.

CHAPTER SEVENTEEN

In 1995, I received a letter from my mother telling me that Salima had died. I know it was a relief that she wasn't saddled with taking total care of my sister, since my ammi was getting older, too. I called her after reading the letter.

"Hi, Ammi," I said as soon as she answered the phone. "I got your letter telling me about Salima. I'm sure she's resting peacefully now with Mahmood."

"Yes, I suppose she is," Ammi replied. "It still hurts to lose her, but mentally she hasn't been with us in over twenty years. It was getting harder for me to take care of her."

"Why don't you and Abba come visit us now? You won't have to rush back home to take care of anyone," I said, hoping they would come stay for a while with us in America.

"I think Bashir and I might visit now. We would love to see all our children and grandchildren again," Ammi said just before hanging up.

Zahid and Husna had moved to Baltimore, Maryland where my other two brothers, Ali and Adnan, were living with their wives. It was a four-hour drive from where I lived, but I would drive there frequently to see them all. I was sure Abba and Ammi would split their time between all of our houses, but I'd have to spend some time in Baltimore when they were in the US for any special events, since so many of our cousins lived there also. In total, about sixty relatives lived in the Baltimore area.

A month later, my parents arrived on vacation. They went to Baltimore first, so Jasim and I took Saba and Hanna to see them. "Have you seen or been in touch with Rashid much since he went back to Pakistan?" I asked Abba as we sat in Zahid's living room sipping tea.

"Yes, we've seen him a few times. He seems content since he and Ahlam got married. She's very happy, too. She said to thank you for such a wonderful husband," Abba said as he winked at me, a smile on his face.

I laughed for a couple of minutes until I realized no one else in the room thought it was funny. I stifled my laugh and excused myself to go into the kitchen with Husna.

I was pleased to hear that Rashid was doing well. I felt sorry for him by then and only wished him the best. And then another chuckle escaped from me as the refrain from an old song came to mind; 'if you can't be with the one you love, honey, love the one you're with'.

I had stopped feeling sorry for myself a long time ago and thought maybe I was supposed to encounter what I'd been through in order to have my daughters whom I adored.

My parents came to New Jersey to visit with us before returning to Pakistan. "Ambreen, I'm so glad you're finally happy now," Ammi said as she pulled me close to her side. "I used to worry about you all the time. I know you had a difficult life with Rashid, and I'm sorry for that. None of us knew he was going to develop a mental illness."

"Thank you, Ammi," I said, choking back the tears that threatened to overflow and spill down my cheeks. Wanting to change the subject, I said, "I'm so happy you and Abba are here for Saba's graduation from college."

"We've been blessed to be able to see all our remaining children and grandchildren," she said as she put water in a kettle to boil for tea.

Abba came into the kitchen and sat on the stool at the counter. "How are my girls doing?" he asked as he looked from my ammi to me.

"Good, Abba," I said, getting up to put tea bags in the cups. "Saba and Hanna are on their way home now. We can go to their favorite restaurant tonight to celebrate."

"That's great," Abba said as he picked up the newspaper and started leafing through it.

After the girls arrived, we went to our favorite Indian restaurant. My parents seemed to really like Jasim and were pleased I had married him. I was so relaxed and had enjoyed the evening so much; I didn't know how I could have ever been any happier at that time.

My parents left to go back to Pakistan, and we settled into a routine of work and leisure in the evenings. I have always liked to read, so much of my time was spent perusing books, particularly biographies. I especially liked books about royals in different countries as they were usually fascinating.

My life with Jasim was pleasant and free from all the hassles I'd been used to in the past. I was thankful he'd rescued me from a solitary, lonely life.

It wasn't long until we got the word that Ammi had cancer. "Hi, Ambreen. I have some news to tell you."

"What's wrong?" I asked with trepidation in my heart.

"I've been diagnosed with bladder cancer, and the doctor here thinks it's already advanced."

"Ammi, you need to come here for treatment," I said as I gripped the phone tightly in my hand. "They are much more advanced here in the USA than they are in Pakistan."

"You're probably right, Ambreen," she said. "Your abba and I have been talking about the possibility of going there for treatment."

Abba took the phone from her and said, "I'm going to make the arrangements for us to go there. I've heard Johns Hopkins Hospital in Baltimore is a wonderful institution for cancer treatments."

"Yes, I've heard that, also," I said. "I look forward to seeing you and Ammi very soon." I hung up with a heavy heart. It would be wonderful to see them again, but I was saddened by the news of my ammi having cancer.

In just a few weeks, my parents arrived in Baltimore, Md., and Ammi began treatment for cancer. I was surprised when I saw my ammi. She'd lost weight and seemed so frail. I suspected she didn't have long to live, so I spent much time going to Baltimore to see her and Abba.

My brothers rallied around her and, if nothing else, kept up her interest in living. We all did our best to stay upbeat around her.

Her chemo treatments were brutal on her, and I felt sad when she was so sick. "I don't know how I can continue these treatments when they make me feel this sick," she said one day after receiving chemo.

"I don't want to lose you, Ammi," I said with tears rolling down my cheeks as I sat down beside her and put my arm around her shoulder, drawing her frail body close to me.

Finally, in 1998, my ammi passed away, and we insisted that she be buried in the Baltimore area. It was a sad day when we planted Ammi in the ground.

Abba stayed for a while and then returned to Pakistan. I don't know why he chose to go back there instead of staying here with his adult children; maybe because his favorite child, Salima, was buried in Pakistan, or maybe because her children were still there. I had a sinking feeling I would have to go there when he died.

I hadn't seen Jabeen in a very long time and wished to see her. I called her and asked why she didn't visit with us. "You can come to New Jersey and stay with Jasim and me," I said, knowing she would go to Baltimore to be with her sister instead.

"I would like to go visit soon. I'll stay with Husna in Baltimore and you can come there," she said. "We'll try to go this summer and see everyone."

I hung up and went to brew a cup of tea. I looked forward to seeing Jabeen again. It had been so long since we'd last met.

The day arrived when I got the call that Jabeen was in Baltimore at Zahid and Husna's house. Jasim and I took off after work on Friday evening and drove there. It was late when we arrived, so everyone had waited for us to have dinner.

Sitting around the dining room table, Jabeen said, "I'm so happy to report that Rashid has gone to Abbottabad and secured a teaching job at the medical college there. He's now a professor of medicine. I'm so proud of him." Her smile seemed to light up her face with pride.

"That's so wonderful. I'm so happy for him," I retorted. "Maybe this is the best thing for him. He certainly wasn't happy here."

"Ahlam says he's like a young child in his enthusiasm for the job," Jabeen said as she pierced a chicken thigh with her fork. "I wish I could see him without going to Pakistan."

Husna smiled and said, "Zahid and I are planning to go visit there sometime in the near future. Why don't you go with us, Jabeen?"

"I wish I could, but I can't be gone from home that long," Jabeen said with a wistful look on her face. "Tell Rashid I pray for him all the time."

"I will," Husna said as she scooped more rice onto her plate and stabbed a piece of apple with her fork.

We enjoyed the weekend with my family members and on Sunday afternoon, we returned to New Jersey. "I'm happy your family is close again," Jasim said as he drove up the Turnpike. "It was unnerving to have everyone at odds with each other."

"Yes, I'm glad, too. It's much more comfortable around the family now." I turned and looked out the window at the landscape as we whizzed past. The sun was beginning to set and the sky was glowing with pink, red and orange colors. It was just stunning. What a beautiful end to the day, I thought.

CHAPTER EIGHTEEN

In 2004, Jasim and I went to India again to visit his family. We toured old castles, forts and palaces. "I can't believe people lived in these places," I said as we climbed up rickety stairs onto the roof of an old fort.

"Yes, it's hard to believe. And to think they had no electricity for lights either," Jasim said as he grabbed my hand to help me on the steps. "They had to use candles to see. Sometimes in large areas, like a castle or palace they would have torches to light the areas."

"I'd have been afraid of using torches for lighting," I said, thinking how easily they could cause a fire.

"Torches probably caused a lot of fires," Jasim said as though reading my mind. "But then there weren't many choices back then."

"I guess that's true. We're lucky to have electricity and gas now." I stepped up onto the roof and looked out over the terrain. It was simply a beautiful landscape. I stood there in awe for several moments before moving on to see other aspects of the fort.

Next on the agenda was the mountain city of Nainital which surrounded a pear-shaped lake. The steep walls of the town's valley were covered with oaks and pines. We took a trip up to the popular hill station of Nainital and were awed at the beauty of the whole area.

Our next stop was Umaid Bhawan Palace which is located in Jodhpur. As we approached the palace, once again, I was awe struck. It is one of the world's largest private residences for the Jodhpur royal family, but contains a hotel which had been awarded the title of World's best hotel, also. The palace is a combination of Indian opulence and Western influence. There is also a museum housed inside the palace.

I learned that the Umaid Bhawan Palace was built between the years 1929 and 1943 and was built to provide employment to thousands of people during the time of famine.

As we walked through the museum I was simply astonished at everything I saw and learned about the palace. Taking Jasim's hand, I said, "This is the most amazing palace I've ever seen."

Jasim seemed to grow in stature as a sense of pride in his Indian heritage overcame him. "Yes, it's absolutely remarkable. The Indians know something special about architecture."

I learned a lot about India that I didn't know. It had always been perceived as the enemy, and I hadn't been interested in knowing much about it. I was totally fascinated by it all then.

Jasim and I returned to the USA, and shortly thereafter, I received notice that my father was gravely ill and would probably not last for very long. I wanted desperately to see him while he was still living. Ali and I decided we'd go together, so we bought our plane tickets and flew to Pakistan.

Abba had developed lung cancer, and the treatments he'd been receiving didn't seem to be slowing the progression of his illness. When I walked into the house and saw how frail he'd become, a lump rose in my throat. I turned to Ali and squeezed his arm.

Sitting in Abba's house were several of our close relatives. I noticed one man sitting nearby who kept glancing at me. I figured he was some distant relative and chose to ignore him.

Finally, one of my other cousins plopped down beside me and said, "Why are you not talking to Rashid?"

"Rashid? Where is he?"

"Right there," she said, indicating the man I'd been ignoring.

"That's him?" I asked incredulously as I stared straight at the heavy-set man who looked nothing like Rashid. "I didn't recognize him. He looks so different from how he used to look."

I got up and moved over to talk with Rashid at that point. Ahlam wasn't with him and I wondered why, but didn't ask. In fact, I didn't ask him much of anything.

"How are you, Rashid?" I asked as I sat down beside him. I noticed that he was twisting his hands together and seemed very nervous. He was also shaking his crossed leg, just slightly, but still very obvious to me.

"I'm fine. How are you?" Rashid turned his head to look me straight in the eyes.

"I'm doing well," I said as I thought about the fact that he didn't stay in touch with his daughters or send any support for them. I was completely surprised that he didn't even ask about his daughters. Maybe he'd put them out of his thoughts, since he couldn't see them now. Perhaps he was one of those men where 'out of sight, out of mind' was his mantra.

I moved back to my original seat and had no more conversation with Rashid. I hoped the best for him, but didn't want any interference with my life because of him.

I stayed a week and visited with Salima's daughter, Farida. I'd always felt close to her and regretted not getting to spend more time with her over the years. Yet, she had opted to stay in Pakistan, and there was no way I would ever want to live there again.

Every morning when I got up, Farida had tea ready and waiting for me along with pieces of fruit. I could get used to this, I thought as I sat down at the table to drink my tea.

"I'm so glad I can spend some extra time with you, Farida," I said as I picked up my teacup and took a sip. The tea was nice and hot, just like I liked it. "I'll hate to leave you again."

"I wish you could stay, too, but I know you have a busy life in America. When I get the chance, I'll go visit you and the rest of the family," Farida said, picking up a piece of apple and biting into it.

"Someday, you may be the only one in the family who's left here. Some of our relatives who still live here are getting older and may not be around much longer," I said, hoping it wouldn't be true. But I did miss Farida very much and would love to see her more often. The fact that my parents had raised her after her mother, Salima, was in the accident made it seem almost like she was my sister.

"Why don't you stay here longer?" Farida asked as she stood up to refill our teacups.

"I'd like to stay and visit longer with you, but I have a job teaching school now," I answered. "I teach little children in kindergarten, and I can't be gone for very long. The substitute teacher I have doesn't work more than a few days a month."

"I'll miss you when you leave, Khala Ambreen," she said, giving me a sad look that almost broke my heart. I loved her so much. The term Khala means Aunt from one's mother's side, whereas Chachi means Aunt on the father's side.

Every day, Farida and I went to see my father and stayed most of the day when he felt up to having us there. Ali was staying with him and kept me updated on how he was when I wasn't around.

A few days later, Ali and I packed our bags and headed home to the USA. At the airport, I looked around and wondered if I'd ever be back. I was torn in a lot of ways; Pakistan was my birthplace and where I grew into a young woman. However, I'd lived in America longer than I'd lived in Pakistan, and it was my home now, and I missed it when I was gone.

As we sat there waiting to board the plane, I reminisced about my life and how it had turned out so differently than I had ever dreamed it would. Finally, we heard the call to board. Getting up, we walked to the jet way to show our tickets.

Once onboard, Ali and I found our seats and settled in for the long flight home. After we'd fastened our seat belts, I adjusted the flow of air from the air conditioning and sat back with eyes closed. I felt such heartache all of a sudden. I knew my abba wouldn't be alive much longer, and suddenly I felt inconsolable. The tears rolled down my cheeks, and I lowered my head so others wouldn't notice.

I thought of Rashid and an overwhelming sense of pity hit me, also. I had cared for him and raised his daughters for so many years, and now I knew I'd probably never see him again. The tears continued to course down my face and drip off my chin.

I heard the jet engines revving and felt the plane begin to back away from the terminal. Soon we were racing down the runway and the plane lifted off the ground. I took a peek out the window as we flew toward the clouds and thought this will be the last time I'll see Pakistan. I had such mixed feelings at that point, I didn't want to think about it anymore, so I lay my head back on the headrest and drifted off to sleep.

When the plane landed in Newark, New Jersey, I was over the melancholy feelings I'd had when I left Pakistan. I undid my seat belt, gathered my personal belongings, and with Ali beside me, walked off the plane with the other passengers.

I was surprised to see Jasim waiting for me in the baggage claim area. Normally, I would have him to pick me up after I got my luggage and had gone out to the curbside.

Rushing toward me, he grabbed me and squeezed. "I'm so happy you're home safe, Ambreen. I've missed you. Are you okay? How was the flight? How are all your relatives in Pakistan?" Jasim said, throwing question after question at me.

"One thing at a time," I said, smiling. "I'm okay and my relatives are all okay. The flight was long, but good. The food was lousy though. I'm hungry for something tasty."

"I have something you like waiting for you at home," Jasim said as he took my luggage and pulled it along behind him. With his other arm, he pulled me close to his side. Suddenly, I felt like I was a valued woman and was glad I had married Jasim.

I felt safe and secure as we drove home, talking about our families. I filled him in on Abba's condition and told Jasim it was near the end for my abba.

About twenty days later, I received word that Abba had passed away. I felt glad I'd gone to see him while he was still living. I knew that he had most likely already been buried.

Since burying the dead the day they die is customary in our culture, none of his adult children could have made it there for the burial. So, we weren't there to witness the funeral prayers of the Muslims in his community. According to our tradition, it is the Muslims collective prayers for the forgiveness of the dead person that grants them absolution.

That night, Jasim held me in his arms to comfort me and when I'd stopped crying, we started making plans for the future.

CHAPTER NINETEEN

Saba moved to her own apartment, and although she was dating a nice doctor, she didn't seem interested in marriage. I wondered if her experience of having a broken home as a child had left her with a bad taste for marriage. I didn't know, and I didn't want to ask her.

Hanna had graduated college and was involved with her work in computers. She'd met a nice young man named Jerry, and after dating for some time, they moved in together. I was very happy with my girls and their chosen careers in life. At least they had choices that I'd never had. They could decide if and when they married and whom they would marry. I wished it had been different for me, too. If only my parents had raised me in this country and let me make my own decision about who to marry, I might have been really happy in life.

Wistful thinking wasn't doing anything for my mental condition, and I didn't want to sink into depression, so I tried to cheer myself up and think only positive things. Every now and then I would think of Shelly and wonder how her life had turned out. I would probably never know.

In 2005, I was sitting in the living room with Jasim, reading a book when the doorbell rang. I got up and answered it. Jerry was standing there with one arm behind his back.

"Come in," I said as I stepped back to allow him to enter. "Where's Hanna?"

"I wanted to see you by myself," he said as he pulled his arm from behind his back and presented me with a beautiful bouquet of flowers. "I'd like to ask for your daughter's hand in marriage."

I was so overcome with emotion that tears sprang up into my eyes, and I could hardly speak. When I recovered, I said, "Of course, Jerry. I'd love to have you as a son-in-law. I'm so happy, I could cry."

Arrangements were made for Hanna and Jerry's wedding. They chose to have it at The Orange County Wedding Estate in New Jersey. The wedding took place outdoors. The surrounding grounds were beautifully decorated with flower covered arches as well as the area for the bride and groom to say their vows.

Hanna was attired in a long white wedding dress with pearls draped around her neck. Her hair was pulled up into a bun at the back of her head. She carried a bouquet of white roses. Hanna looked simply gorgeous and my heart was bursting with pride.

Jerry was Catholic, and so they had a priest to marry them. As soon as they said their vows, pictures were taken. Since there was only immediate family present, it was a small affair.

We walked to the reception hall after the pictures were taken. When I entered the room, I noticed how lovely everything looked. The tables were decorated with vases of white, pink and yellow flowers, and each table had an ornamental candle on it.

Hanna beamed with happiness during the reception dinner. I kept looking at her and thinking how happy I was that my youngest child was married to the man she loved.

A few years later, Hanna gave birth to a daughter, Sydney, and a couple of years after that, she gave birth to another daughter, Julia. I absolutely loved being a grandmother. I couldn't wait to see them and all my thoughts centered on my granddaughters. My life was good at last, I thought.

Always looking for a new adventure, Saba and I made plans to travel to Europe. We flew to Budapest, Hungary, one of the most beautiful cities in Europe. Located on the Danube River, it has many museums and galleries such as the Museum of Fine Arts, Franz Liszt Academy of Music, Hungarian National Museum and the House of Terror. I wasn't sure I wanted to tour the House of Terror, though.

The central area of the city along the Danube River has many notable monuments. Some of them include Buda Castle, Gresham Palace, Fisherman's Bastion and the Szechenyi Chain Bridge.

Budapest is home to the second-oldest metro line in the world, the Millennium Underground Railway. Both of my girls had inherited my sense of adventure and loved to travel, also. Saba and I went exploring every day to see as many of the wonders that Hungary had to offer.

We visited the Roman settlement, Aquincum, which was built in 106AD. Today this area corresponds to the Obuda district which is located in Budapest. This archaeological site was turned into a museum with some open-air sections.

Since we were close to Vienna, Austria, we took a day trip there to explore that city. Traveling by rail, we enjoyed seeing the countryside. After returning to Budapest, we returned home to the USA with our pictures and memories.

CHAPTER TWENTY

April, 2014

Another big shock in my life occurred when I returned home from teaching kindergartners and Jasim greeted me in the kitchen. "Rashid's son-in-law called for you today," he said as he handed me a piece of paper with a phone number on it.

"What do you mean; Rashid's son-in-law?" I asked, a puzzled look on my face. "Do you mean Jerry?" I couldn't understand why Jasim would refer to Jerry as Rashid's son-in-law instead of mine.

"No, not Jerry. I didn't catch his name, but he asked for you to call back when you got home." Jasim hadn't yet put together that Rashid possibly had another son-in-law; the husband of Anita.

I was just beginning to think of such a possibility myself, so I took out my cell phone and called the number which was on the paper. When a woman answered the phone, I said, "Someone called for me from this number today."

"Ambreen?"

"Yes, this is Ambreen. Who am I talking to," I said, wondering if it was Anita.

"This is Shelly. Do you remember me?"

"Of course, I remember you, Shelly. How could I ever forget you?" I was stunned to hear from the woman I'd worried about for so many years.

"I found your phone number on a website and thought I'd contact you. It would be nice if our daughters could get to know each other. I didn't know you were in the United States. I thought you'd taken the girls and gone back to Pakistan after your divorce," Shelly said with excitement in her voice.

"No, we've been here since the early eighties," I said. "Why did you think we were in Pakistan?" I was curious to know why she had thought we'd gone back to Pakistan. And how did she know Rashid and I were divorced? I wondered.

"Rashid called me in 1989 and then again in 1992. He told me he was divorced, and when I asked him where you were, he said you'd taken the girls and gone back to Pakistan."

I wondered why Rashid would tell Shelly that the girls and I were in Pakistan. It made no sense to me. "Are you sure he said we'd gone to Pakistan?"

"Yes, he said he was in New York on his way to Canada, and you were in Pakistan. In fact, he said he'd been working in Sudan and was going to Ethiopia. He said he'd become a missionary doctor."

Wow, the lies he'd told Shelly were astronomical. He'd never worked in Sudan or anywhere else in Africa. I was surprised to learn he'd called her in 1992, around the time of our divorce. I knew he'd called in 1989, but thought he'd given up wanting to talk to her.

"He did go to Egypt for a couple of weeks around that time. Maybe that's what he was referring to," I said as I wondered if he thought he'd been working there. With his mental illness, who knew what he conjured up in his mind?

"Until I read about him on the website I found, I thought maybe he was dead because I've not heard from him for so long. Then

I read that he'd gone back to Pakistan and remarried a third time, to another cousin," she said. "I was completely surprised to read the statement that said he'd gone to the US and England for further studies and had married a white American. I told Anita and her husband, Sean, 'oh my gosh, that's me'." Shelly laughed and her laughter was contagious. I found myself laughing with her.

"So how often did he contact you?" I asked, not out of jealousy because I was over that, but simply curiosity.

"The first time I got a letter from him after you and he left Canada was in November, 1978. It was mailed from somewhere around Indus River in Pakistan. I wrote back to him and told him I was remarried. I told him not to write to me again. My present husband wouldn't like it. I suggested that he write to his daughter, Anita, instead. So, he and Anita wrote to each other at least once."

I was surprised to learn he'd written to Shelly from the Indus River area. He'd certainly kept that a secret. I immediately thought of the locked desk drawer in his office and realized he must have kept their letters in it.

"Do you still live in California?" I asked. "I'd tried to call you sometime in the nineties and talked to some man who said you lived in California."

"Yes, I do. We all live here. You must have called my dad and talked to him. Rashid always called mom and dad when he wanted to get hold of me. The website I saw said you live in New Jersey. Do you live close to Newark?"

"Yes, very close to there."

"Well, I've got a lot of things to take care of tonight, but call me again soon, so we call talk more. I'm so happy to finally connect with you, Ambreen," she said. "Maybe someday we can meet in person."

"Yes, I'd like to meet you, too. Is there a good time for me to call you, since there's a three-hour difference?" I asked.

"I'm usually home after three o'clock most days, and I go to bed around nine. I'm still working part time, and I have to get up very early on the days I work. So, if you call around seven, it would be four here, and that would be good timing. Or try whenever; I could be off and at home," Shelly said.

"I'm so glad you contacted me, Shelly. Finally, we can talk and bare our souls to each other," I said, thinking about all the things Rashid had told me that I could now ask Shelly. "Are you on Facebook? I'll send you a friend request, if you are."

"Yes, I am. Also, give me your email address and we can email pictures, etcetera," Shelly said.

"What's your last name now?" I asked since I knew she'd been remarried.

"I took my maiden name back, so I'm once again Shelly Sinclair. I couldn't see hanging onto a married name when I'd divorced the man whose name it was," Shelly said with a chuckle before hanging up.

Eager to see her, I waited for the email she promised to send. I was so glad that, finally, I was going to get to see what Shelly looked like, since she promised to send me an early picture of her and Rashid. They'd had it taken to give to their parents. According to what Rashid told Shelly, his mother cut her out of the picture and framed Rashid's face. I wondered if that was the picture they had sent to me when asking me to marry him.

The following day, I could hardly wait to call Shelly again. I'm not even sure what all we talked about at that time, but we rehashed all of our young years with Rashid.

"Rashid told me you were a student nurse when he met you," I said on one of our many calls to each other. "How did you end up dating him?"

Shelly laughed and I assumed she must be remembering something humorous. "We saw each other in the hospital cafeteria and smiled. Two days later, a friend of his called and asked if it was okay for Rashid to call me. He said Rashid wanted to ask me on a date. I said 'yes' and as soon as I hung up, the phone rang again, and it was Rashid calling to ask me out. I said yes, of course, and on Friday evening of that week, we went out to dinner and a movie."

I was amazed at the revelation that Rashid was the one who initiated dating Shelly. He'd led me to believe some doctor friends had fixed him up with her, when in fact, he'd seen her and was interested.

"Did you know he'd been engaged to my sister, Salima?" I asked, wondering if he'd revealed that to her.

"Yes. Rashid told me he'd been engaged since birth to his cousin. He explained that marriages were arranged at an early age in Pakistan. He told me she ran off and married someone else, so he was off the hook."

"Did he date anyone else besides you?" I asked as I thought maybe he'd had other women during that time. I had the impression he was very suave and debonair with the ladies from some of his stories.

"Not that I ever knew about," Shelly said. "If he saw someone else, it was a well-kept secret, since I saw him almost daily at the hospital and in the evenings when some of us student nurses and resident doctors gathered to play ping pong and watch television shows. And, of course, every weekend, we were out on dates. Usually we'd go to dinner and a movie. Sometimes we'd walk around the downtown area before coming back to our dorms which were side by side across the street from the hospital."

"So, you probably would have known if he was dating someone else, too," I said.

"I think he had gone out on a date with someone who worked in the lab before he met me," Shelly said. "If I remember correctly, he told me that it was only one date, though."

I still didn't know what she looked like and it had bothered me for years. "So why didn't you send me a picture of yourself when you sent Anita's picture to me? I sent you one of my pictures," I said.

"I didn't want you to see what I looked like, because when I saw how pretty you were, I felt so ugly," Shelly admitted.

"Have you emailed the picture of you and Rashid yet?" I asked, hoping she'd send it right away.

"I'll send it as soon as we hang up. I promise," she said.

We talked about our daughters and hoped to get them talking to each other. Both of us were grandmothers by then, and I was surprised to learn that Shelly was also a great grandmother. She had two small great grandsons. So, Anita had already become a grandmother, too, and I wondered if Rashid realized he was a great grandfather. It probably never entered his mind.

How sad it is that Anita, her children and grandchildren had never gotten to know Rashid, I thought as Shelly and I talked. It was a tragedy for them as well as for Rashid. I had come to blame his father primarily. If he hadn't coerced Rashid into divorcing Shelly, everyone might have had a happy life. But then again, who knew for sure; only God knew, and I had my daughters to be grateful for as well. For without that turn of event, they wouldn't have been born.

Mother's Day arrived and I called Shelly to wish her a Happy Mother's Day. We talked about what we were doing that day, and then I said, "When can we meet? Our daughters should meet, also."

"That's a great idea. Maybe we could meet somewhere," Shelly said. "I'll be going to West Virginia the end of July for my 50th high school class reunion, and the following week, my aunt turns 100. We're having a big party for her. She's my dad's oldest sister and the only one of his siblings still living. My dad passed away two years ago."

"Maybe we could meet halfway, say in Baltimore. My brothers all live there and we could meet at Zahid's house."

"That would actually work out very well," Shelly said. "I could drive there and meet you. I'll let you know the exact date later, but it should be somewhere around the beginning of August."

"I'm so glad we'll be able to meet," I said. "I'm thankful you contacted me, Shelly. I think it was meant for us to finally get acquainted."

"Yes, I think so, too. I believe there is a purpose for us getting to know each other," she said.

The next couple of months flew by, and before I knew it, August was upon us. Shelly and I had made arrangements to meet at Zahid's house. Anita, Saba and Hanna had been talking to each other, and it was agreed among them that Anita, her husband and their oldest son would fly to New Jersey to meet at Hanna's house. Saba would join them there, and they would all drive to Baltimore to meet the rest of the family.

I had given Shelly the address, and she informed me she'd made arrangements to stay at a nearby hotel. Jasim and I drove to Baltimore in anticipation of meeting her and Anita. I was excited when the big day arrived at last. Of course, she'd sent me pictures of herself when she was young, so I already knew what she had looked like. And I'd seen her pictures on Facebook, too.

When Shelly knocked on the door at Zahid's house, I dashed to the door and opened it. I was surprised that Shelly was a few inches taller than me. She had grayish blond hair and big brown eyes. Although our eyes weren't exactly alike, we both had big eyes. I could see why Rashid said our foreheads were similar though.

Smiling, we embraced each other. "Come in," I said, taking a hold of her arm to guide her into Zahid's house. My brother and his family all came to the door behind me and welcomed Shelly with hugs.

I was somewhat surprised when Shelly clung to my side at first. I suppose she was nervous meeting some of Rashid's relatives for the first time. That was understandable, since his parents disapproved of his marriage to her. Perhaps she felt that all his family would not approve of it either and not be kind to her, I thought as I watched her closely.

When we sat down on the sofa, Shelly grabbed my arm and stayed close to my side. Soon, Hanna, Saba and Anita showed up with husbands and children. Anita's son was a young man of twenty-nine. I could see a resemblance to Rashid when I looked at Steven. A young Rashid, I thought as I scrutinized him closely.

I learned that night that Shelly and I had more in common than simply having been married to Rashid. We both loved to travel, and adventure was in our blood. We were posing for pictures with our daughters when Hanna said, "Why don't you and my mother travel together, Shelly? She needs someone to go places with and since you like to travel it would be good for you both."

Shelly looked at me and said, "I could possibly travel with you next year, if you want to go somewhere."

"That would be wonderful. Let's think about it and maybe plan a trip."

"I'm going to go see you in New Jersey this fall," Shelly said as she picked up her glass of water and took a sip. "I'll go for a long weekend, and we can talk the night away."

"Good. Just let me know when you want to come," I said, feeling like I'd made a friend for life. I reflected back to the time I received a kind letter from her years ago and thought I'd like her, if I had met her under different circumstances. My instinct had been right. I did like this woman I used to be jealous of because of Rashid.

Over dinner, a comment was made about the fact that Rashid had gone to Pakistan and married me while still legally married to Shelly. "Well, I guess that made us sister-wives. That's what the Mormons call women who are married to the same man at the same time," she said, laughing.

I laughed, too. It was a funny concept then. Of course, it hadn't been so funny at the time it happened though. Shelly and I started calling each other sister after that. We had a bond that others either didn't understand, or chose to ignore. We were the mothers of Rashid's daughters, for one thing, and that gave us reason to feel connected.

The entire group posed for a photo. I don't remember who took the picture, but it was most likely Zahid and Husna's son-in-law. I told Shelly we should send the picture to Rashid. She agreed and said she'd write him a letter of forgiveness and understanding and would include the picture. However, later on, we decided it wouldn't be a good idea, since it could cause Rashid much anguish.

Sometime during the evening, I felt in a joking mood and said to Shelly, "You know you ruined my honeymoon by calling."

"And you ruined my marriage by marrying Rashid," she retorted and we both laughed.

Several hours later, Shelly, Anita, Sean and Steven said goodnight and left for their hotel rooms. I wanted to spend more time with them, but knew it would have to wait for another time.

As Shelly was saying goodnight to everyone, she commented to me, "It's strange all your brothers have moved to Baltimore. This is where I was born."

"Really? This is your birthplace?"

"Yes, it is. I lived in Baltimore until around the age of five when my parents decided to return to their home state of West Virginia," Shelly said as she waved at me.

I watched as they strode down the walkway and got in their cars. I would have to talk to her on the phone again before we could spend more time in person.

Jasim and I returned to New Jersey the next day. The following week, Zahid called and said he'd talked to Rashid who was still living in Pakistan. He'd told him about our meeting with Shelly and

Anita. Rashid had said, 'Oh, boy! How did this happen?' I'm sure he never dreamed his two ex-wives would ever meet.

Now that he was married to a third wife, he probably didn't want her thinking about his first two ex-wives, I thought after I hung up from talking to my brother.

Over the months we'd been talking to each other, I discovered we genuinely liked one another, and I began looking forward to talking to Shelly often. It was like having a close sister in my life; someone I could share things with who totally understood me and all I'd been through.

When I'd listened to the details of Shelly Sinclair's life, I realized the events in her life weren't really any better than mine. I was beginning to feel a closeness to Shelly that I didn't have with anyone else.

CHAPTER TWENTY-ONE

On a Thursday in October, 2014, Shelly came to New Jersey to visit me. I took my neighbor and close friend, Rose, and drove to Newark to pick her up from the airport. Jasim was in India at the time and would be gone for about six months. He was dealing with the courts concerning a house he owned there in New Delhi.

Shelly emerged from the airport towing her luggage behind her. I pulled alongside the curb, got out, helped put her suitcase in the trunk and hugged her. "Are you hungry?" I asked as soon as she got in the back seat and buckled up. "Rose and I want to stop at Dunkin Donuts for a coffee," I said as soon as I had introduced them.

"That's fine. I could use a cup of coffee, too," Shelly said. She answered the questions Rose asked her, and they seemed to get along just fine. I had already told her that Rose would make cappuccino for her in the morning while I worked and would take her to Saba's house for lunch. I would meet them there.

When we got to the house, I showed Shelly where she would sleep. She stashed her suitcase in the room, and when she returned, she presented two books to me as a gift. We had talked about the fact we both loved to read. We were enthusiastic about history, so historical fiction was one of the types of books we liked.

We were getting hungry, so we went into the kitchen to get the food out for dinner. I had already cooked Indian food, which I knew Shelly liked, so we just had to heat it up.

Not knowing what she preferred, I had a whole chicken. I laughed to myself as I watched Shelly pick out only the chicken breast which was my favorite also. "So, you don't like the legs or thighs?" I asked as I scooped salad onto my plate.

"No. The meat on them is too slimy for my taste," Shelly said, smiling as she cut into the meat.

Laughing, I said, "Well, that's another thing we have in common."

We talked for a while and then got ready for bed. When I arose the next morning, Shelly was still sleeping. I found it incredible that the day had arrived that she and I would become friends and visit together.

I left for work just as she was getting out of bed. I met Rose on the sidewalk going to my house. I was confident that Shelly would have a great cup of cappuccino at breakfast and would go to lunch somewhere with Rose.

Around one o'clock I left work and drove to Saba's house. Shelly and Rose were already there. Saba and Norman had picked up Indian food, and although Rose had stopped at a fast food place so she and Shelly could have lunch, we all had some of the food Saba had on her kitchen table.

That evening after dinner, Shelly and I sat in my living room and talked until it was quite late. We'd made plans to go to New York and needed to get up early to catch the bus, so we said goodnight.

By that time, I felt like I'd known Shelly very well for years as we talked about our lives and what had happened to each of us.

On Saturday morning, we ate a light breakfast and got ready to leave for the bus stop. When the bus arrived, we sat in the front seats. On the way to Manhattan, we talked and laughed so much, the bus driver turned and scowled at us.

We met Shelly's friend, Elizabeth and her daughter at the bus station. "I'm so glad you could meet us," Shelly said as she hugged them both. "I've missed you since you left San Diego."

"I've missed you, too," Elizabeth said as she took Shelly by the arm and started across the street. "There's a good place to eat a few blocks away." Elizabeth was a short woman from the Philippines. Her jet-black hair was cut short in a bob. Her teenage daughter looked like she was half white and was very beautiful. I kept looking at her features and thinking she could be a movie star.

"Okay. Since you know the area, lead us there," Shelly said, looking back to make sure I was following with Elizabeth's daughter. We walked several blocks to the restaurant for lunch. I enjoyed meeting her friend. After lunch, we walked to the subway and rode a train to ground zero. We strode around the area taking pictures.

"Wow, this is certainly big," Shelly said as she peered over the wall. "Such a tragedy."

"Yes, it was," I said as I wondered if all the adherents to my faith were being blamed. To make sure Shelly and her friends knew I didn't belong to the same group as the terrorists, I said, "I'm glad my sect doesn't believe in this type of Jihad."

Elizabeth and her daughter looked at me and smiled. I felt better immediately.

Looking at my watch, I said, "It's almost time for our bus. We should head back."

"Okay, I'm ready," Shelly said as she stepped up to walk beside her friend. I walked along with her friend's daughter. What a beautiful girl, I thought again as I glanced at her.

When we arrived at the terminal, we said goodbye to Elizabeth and her daughter. We still had a little while to wait on the bus back to New Jersey. Finally, it arrived and we boarded, sitting away from the driver in case we found something humorous to laugh about.

When we got back to New Jersey, we decided to go out to an Indian restaurant for dinner. After we were seated, we waited for a long time to be served. We finally got our food and then rushed home. We went into the living room and sat on the sofa to talk.

"Would you like to go to Prague next spring?" I asked with a hopeful look on my face. "It would need to be the week of Spring break for me.

"Yes, I'd love to go," Shelly replied as she dug out her tablet and looked at a website for flights to Prague as I pulled out my calendar and we got the dates.

"Here's a really good price for airfare and hotel." She showed me the webpage.

"That's great," I said, astonished that she had found such good rates so quickly.

"Should I go ahead and book it now? I can put it on my credit card and you can send me a check for your fare," Shelly said, looking up from her tablet.

"Yes, book it," I said. I was so happy to have someone I liked as a travel companion. Over the months that Shelly and I had been getting better acquainted and after visiting, I discovered that I liked her immensely. She was easy going, but mostly, I liked the fact that she was very sweet and loving. At last, I could understand why Rashid had been so taken with her.

Shelly's plane didn't leave for California until late afternoon, so she wanted to go to church Sunday morning, since she is a devout Christian. I drove to a church close to where Saba lived and we went in. Unfortunately, we were too late for the service and had arrived during the last song.

We ate lunch and then I dropped her off at the airport. "I'll see you in March, my friend," Shelly said as she took her suitcase and gave me a hug. "I'm looking forward to traveling with you."

As I drove home I wished we lived close to each other, so we could visit often. We'd been thrown together by odd circumstances, but we'd overcome any obstacles in forging a true, loving friendship. It goes to show you how people from different parts of the world can be so much alike, I thought when I considered all Shelly and I had in common, our likes and dislikes.

Getting ready for bed that night, I realized I missed Shelly and her laughter. She had the uncanny ability to make me laugh with her. I slipped under the covers and turned out the light. It would only be a few months until our trip to the Czech Republic.

As we neared the end of the year and our upcoming trip grew closer, our conversations started being more about what we wanted to see in Prague, how we would travel around the city once we were there and what all we planned to take. Shelly was afraid it would be bitterly cold that time of year in Europe, so she was planning to take some heavy sweaters and jackets. I figured it would be warm and pleasant and we'd just need lightweight sweaters and thin clothing.

CHAPTER TWENTY-TWO

On January 25, 2015, I received a call from my brother Zahid. "Rashid died today. He was coming out of the bedroom and had a heart attack. It killed him instantly," he said, his voice choked with emotion.

"Oh, no," I said as the tears began to flow. I sobbed until I couldn't think straight. We talked for a while and then hung up. I'm not sure how much I talked as I was crying so hard. Even though we had been divorced for over twenty years, it still hurt to hear that he had died.

I called Shelly as soon as I could. "Shelly, I have some bad news to tell you. Rashid died today," I said, my voice breaking.

"I'm so sorry to hear that. What happened to him?" she asked with sympathy in her voice.

"Heart attack," I said. "I had to call and let you know immediately. You're the only one who would know how I feel." I was still crying between sentences.

"I do understand and I'm so sorry, Ambreen. But I have cried over him so much, I don't have a lot of tears left now. I grieved for him many years ago when I lost him. I loved him so much and he was ripped away from me when Anita was a baby." Shelly may have said she had no tears left, but I could hear her crying softly. Her voice was filled with tears when she spoke again, "Have you talked to number three yet." Shelly and I had jokingly begun to call his current wife 'number three'.

"Yes, I called and gave her my condolences. She is very depressed right now. She's still a relatively young woman, you know. Rashid was twenty-five years older than her."

"Wow, she's barely older than Anita. I didn't realize she was so young," Shelly said. "That's young to become a widow. She could have many years of loneliness ahead of her."

"Yes, she could, indeed," I said. "Well, I need to get ready for bed, so I'll talk to you soon." I hung up feeling a little better for having shared my feelings with Shelly.

Toward the end of March, 2015, Shelly once again came to New Jersey. It was the day before our trip to Prague. Jasim was still in India, so she spent the day with Rose while I worked half a day.

When I returned from the school, I was exhausted after dealing with a classroom of kindergartners. I packed my last-minute items and called my friend who had offered to drive us to the airport. We were waiting by the door when my friend arrived.

We were dropped off at the airport in Newark, N.J. two hours before departure. After we checked in and went to our gate, we sat talking about our grandchildren and Shelly's great grandchildren. All three of her grandchildren were now adults. Her granddaughter, Natalie, would be graduating from college in just a few months. "I find it hard to believe it's already been four years since she started to college," Shelly said, laughing. "Time is just zipping right by."

"Yes, it certainly is," I replied. "When I think of all the years we've missed out on because of stupid jealousy, I regret feeling that way."

"So do I," Shelly said. "We should've stayed in touch back in the beginning when we were first writing to each other. Then our daughters would have gotten to know each other a lot sooner."

It was finally time to board the plane. We were flying on Delta Airlines and would have to change planes in Amsterdam. We took our seats and buckled up, stowing our purses under the seat in front of us.

The plane backed out and turned toward the runway. We sat there for a few minutes while the pilots revved the engines, and I suppose, did their final checks. Then we proceeded to the runway and turned onto it. I felt myself become tense and hoped Shelly didn't notice.

As soon as we started down the runway, I grabbed the armrests tightly in my clutch. My whole body was rigid. Even though I'd flown many times, I feared take-offs, because they seemed so scary when leaving the ground and aiming toward the clouds.

Shelly reached over and took my hand. "Are you scared?" she asked as her other hand encircled our joined hands.

"Yes. I don't like this part of flying," I responded, still feeling tense.

"Don't be afraid," she said, leaning over close to me. "We'll be alright. We're in God's hands and He will keep us safe. I just feel it."

At that moment, I began to calm down. Shelly's faith portrayed itself in calm assurance and therefore her reassuring words gave me a sense of peace that I'd not known before when flying. At that moment, I wished I could always have Shelly with me when I fly.

As soon as we were up in the clouds, she released my hand and looked out the window. It was getting dark, so she closed the shade.

Dinner was served, and after we ate, Shelly began to feel sick. She'd eaten the salad, but I hadn't. I could see her struggling to hang onto the seat backs as she made her way up the aisle to the restroom. It seemed quite a while had passed, and she still wasn't back. I unbuckled my seatbelt to go check on her, when I saw her walking back down the aisle.

When she was once again seated, I asked, "Are you feeling okay now?"

"Yes, I'm better, thanks. I felt like I was going to pass out. I broke out in a cold sweat, and after a short while, the feeling passed." She re-buckled her seat belt and leaned back to relax and sleep.

When we descended into Amsterdam, I was glad that the first leg of our flight was over. We would have eight hours at the airport before our flight left for Prague.

Once in the airport, we drank coffee and wandered around from shop to shop, looking for souvenirs from The Netherlands. We purchased a few things, and then sat down to read. It seemed like a very long eight hours waiting in an airport. But it also seemed like the prime time to question Shelly about some things I'd always wondered about.

"I found a light-colored hair pin in one of the twin beds in Rashid's apartment when I first moved to New York," I said. "Had you been there, and was it your hair pin?"

"Twin beds? I thought it was one bed," Shelly said, looking pensive. "If they were twins, then he had them together."

"So, you were there?" I asked, turning to look her in the eyes.

"Yes, I spent a week in New York with Rashid in January, 1970. We were going through a divorce, and he came to West Virginia almost every weekend to see me and Anita. So, we decided I should go to New York for a week, since I'd never been there," Shelly said. "As far as the hair pin, maybe it was mine. I don't remember. We used to wear curlers at night, but I'm not sure if I'd ever worn them when sleeping with Rashid; I don't think I did." She laughed heartily. "If I did, maybe that's why he agreed to divorce me." She laughed even louder at that joke.

"Do you think he had another girlfriend after you, but before me?" I asked.

"I don't know. It's possible, I guess. I did find a woman's watch in the living room of his apartment in New York when I was cleaning, and I asked him about it. He told me he'd bought it for you."

"Well, he never gave it to me," I said as I looked at the time to see if we should get to our gate for the plane to Prague. We still had lots of time left.

Shelly laughed again. "Well, that's because he gave it to me. He told me if I wanted it, I could have it, so I took it."

"Well, you owe me a watch," I said, laughing.

"Ambreen, someday I'm going to buy a watch for you." Shelly smiled at me.

"Did he take you sight-seeing while you were there?" I asked, wondering if they had spent all their time in bed. To think I was in Pakistan waiting for my husband to summon me to New York, and he was spending time in New York with his first wife, I thought as I mulled it over in my mind.

"Of course, he took me to see the Statue of Liberty, the Empire State Building, Times Square and Rockefeller Center where there was an ice skating rink and huge Christmas tree. He also took me to Tiffany's."

"Everywhere he took you, he also took me," I said. "He must have been reliving his past with you when he took me to those places."

"He was working during most of the days when I was there, so I did a lot of cleaning while I waited for him to come home," Shelly said. "His bathroom was especially dirty and I couldn't stand it, so I scrubbed it really well."

"Thanks," I said, laughing. "It wasn't too bad when I arrived there."

"You're welcome, although he must have cleaned it again before you arrived, since you didn't get there until March."

"I don't know if he did or not. He wasn't very domestic in that sense," I said, remembering some of his messes I'd had to clean up.

"Let's go get a coffee, so we can stay awake," Shelly said as she popped up off the chair and started to walk towards a café.

I followed along after her, and after we purchased our coffee, we found a table and sat down to drink them. I still had more questions, but didn't want to appear too nosy. My curiosity got the best of me, and I asked, "When you went to New York, did he meet you at the airport?" I was remembering when I first arrived in New York and had trouble finding him. I had already told that story to Shelly.

"Funny you should ask," Shelly said. "My flight was into LaGuardia and when I got my luggage, I couldn't find Rashid. So, I hired a taxi and went to his apartment. When I got to his door, he opened it and welcomed me with a hug. I said 'Why didn't you go to the airport to meet me?' and he said 'I'm cooking dinner for you and couldn't leave'."

"He cooked dinner for you?" I asked, incredulously. He had never done anything except boil eggs to my knowledge.

"Yes, he made chicken curry. He had a big pot on the stove and it smelled really good. But when we sat down to eat, I was a little hesitant, because he'd become mentally ill, and I didn't know if it was safe to eat or not. After he took a bite, I decided to go ahead and eat. I have to say, it was rather tasty." Shelly had a faraway look in her eyes as she was remembering her time in New York.

Finally, we were able to board our flight to Prague. It would only take a couple of hours to get there. We settled back in our seats and resumed talking. "You said you went to London to be with him. How was he when you were there?" I asked.

"He was wonderful at that time. He came to the airport and met me. We took a cab to where he was staying and later we checked into a bed and breakfast place, but we didn't care much for it. So, we found a hotel near Piccadilly Circus and stayed there the rest of the time I was in London. We had a fabulous time." Shelly accepted a cup of coffee from the flight attendant.

"Where did he take you? Did you get to see all the sights?" I asked, remembering when he and I were in London to visit relatives.

"He took me to see all the important sights in London; Westminster Abbey, Buckingham Palace. We went into the queen's gallery at the palace and saw the royal art work as well as the horses' saddles of different kings. We toured The Tower of London and saw the torture chambers as well as the crown jewels. I don't think we missed anything on the tours we did.

"We took a boat ride down the Thames River, went to a show, saw the Natural History Museum, went to Madam Tussad's Wax Museum and visited Charles Dickens house. He introduced me to Indian food, which I loved. We had a wonderful time when I was there," Shelly said and then looked out the window. "We bought a bottle of port wine and drank a little of it at night before we went to bed. We were trying to find a wine we liked."

"I see. I feel like everywhere he took you, he took me when we were there. I wonder if he thought of you when we were touring those places, too," I said, looking at Shelly.

"Now don't be jealous," Shelly said, laughing. "After all, it was a long time ago and you were with him much longer than I was. But he was very kind and attentive to me when we were together. He seemed to love me quite a lot back then."

I laughed and said, "No, I'm not jealous anymore. Too much time has passed and you're right, it was a long, long time ago."

"Look, we're almost at the airport. I can see the city in the distance," Shelly said as we felt the plane turning and descending to land.

The plane landed smoothly in Prague and taxied to the gate. We got off the plane and went to claim our luggage. We trudged out to the curb where we found our ride which we had already arranged to take us to our hotel in Prague. It seemed a long drive there, but when we arrived, we were pleased with the location.

Our lodging was called the Orea Hotel Pyramida which is minutes from the historic city center of Prague. The hotel was obviously named Pyramida because it resembled a pyramid. The tram ran right in front of the hotel, and there was a ticket machine just outside the entrance of the hotel, as well as an ATM. We were happy to see that we would not have any trouble getting around to various places while staying there.

After checking in, we took our room keys and got on the elevator. We were on the fourth floor, and the window overlooked a side street. The room was small with two twin beds. We were both pleased to see that the toilet was separate from the sink and shower stall.

We ate dinner in the Bohemia restaurant which was located on the ground floor in the back section of the hotel. The soup was very good and the bread was tasty.

Afterwards, we wandered around looking at where the pool and sauna were located. Since we were tired from the long journey, we went back to our room and got ready for bed early.

Propped up on our beds, we talked for a while. I had always wanted to know more about Shelly's call the first time I'd ever talked to her. I decided now was a good time to ask her. "When you called the first time and told me who you were, I wondered why Rashid was sending you money. Later, when I found out about Anita, I knew why he needed to send it, but he never let me know how much he had to send," I said as I fluffed the pillow behind my back.

"Oh, he was supposed to send fifty dollars a month for Anita's support. He did send it for almost a year, and then he wrote saying he couldn't send anymore because you and he were going back to Pakistan." Shelly pulled the covers up over her chest.

"When he and I divorced, he was supposed to send fifty dollars a month to me, also. Twenty-five for each girl," I said. "But he never did send it to me."

"Maybe because he kept going back to Pakistan," Shelly said, chuckling.

I started laughing, too, and then we were both howling with laughter. "I suppose his mental state had a lot to do with his inability to take care of his girls financially," I said. "It's okay, though."

"Yes, I'm sure that had a lot to do with it," Shelly said. "I wonder if he suffered guilt feelings over it."

"We'll never know now," I said, snuggling down in the bed to go to sleep.

"Goodnight, my friend. I'm so glad we met and that we both love to travel," Shelly said as she reached over and turned off the lamp in our room.

"Yes, me, too. Night," I said and laid my head back on the pillow and closed my eyes.

In the morning, we dressed and made our way down to the restaurant. After eating breakfast, we grabbed our coats from our rooms and went out to buy our tickets for the tram to the downtown area. There were a few people waiting at the stop, so we joined them. Map in hand, we tried to figure where to get off in order to meet our tour guide. We had signed up for a walking tour of Prague online before we left the USA.

Not knowing where to get off, we disembarked at the wrong place, but several very nice people pointed us in the right direction.

Finally, we found the street where the tour office was located and hooked up with our guide.

It started off being a walking tour as we were shown places we had read about during the Communist regime. Meandering along the cobbled streets of medieval Old Town, we passed by the old clock tower which was spectacular. Amazed at such intricacies, we snapped several pictures of it.

Next, we were taken through the old Jewish Quarter and learned of its troubled past during World War II. It was amazing to be standing in a spot that we had read about years ago.

Ending up by the river, we boarded a small river boat, so we could observe the city from a different perspective. We were offered a drink, and I chose cappuccino while Shelly had a glass of red wine. Looking out the window, we saw lovely sights along the Vltava River.

When the cruise was over, we were taken to a 17th-century tavern for lunch. The food was good and we got acquainted with some of our fellow tourists.

Our guide led us to a tram station and gave us tickets. "We are going to ride up the hill to Prague Castle," she said as she made sure we all entered the tram. It had started to rain, and luckily, Shelly had brought an umbrella with her. I got on, and she followed as soon as she put her umbrella down. Our tickets had gotten wet and the machine inside the tram wouldn't take them. We just shrugged our shoulders and took our seats before the tram started moving.

The Prague Castle with its fairy-tale façade overlooked the city. We were all busy snapping photos until it was time to walk back down the hill and cross the famous Charles Bridge with its many statues.

Shelly and I were enthralled with the enchanting atmosphere of Prague with its rich cultural traditions. We had enjoyed the tour immensely and hoped we could do more sight-seeing while in the Czech Republic.

When we arrived back in our hotel room, Shelly went to the window and looked out. "Look. See the old building straight across from us. That's Prague Castle."

"I didn't know we were so close to it," I said. "It's definitely within walking distance."

Every day after breakfast, we ventured out to explore the city and dine on their cuisine. Walking along the street, looking at souvenirs, I started to laugh.

"Shelly, if I'd known you were so easy to get along with and so likeable, we could have both stayed married to Rashid at the same time. Then we could have traveled while he worked," I said, joking, but also letting her know how much I liked her.

Shelly laughed so hard that tears sprang to her eyes. "Yes, we could have been traveling the world for many decades, if not for our jealousy." She put her arm around my shoulder as we walked along toward the next vendor. "I'm so happy we finally met and became friends."

"So am I," I said, smiling. "When I first found out you'd been married to Rashid, I felt like I was intruding in your marriage. Didn't you hate me for that?"

"No, I never hated you. In fact, I never blamed you at all, because I knew you were innocent in what happened." Shelly smiled broadly with understanding in her eyes. "The only people I ever blamed were Rashid's parents. After he told me they disapproved of our marriage and ordered him to divorce me, I sent them pictures of Anita. I thought maybe, if they saw their granddaughter, they would allow Rashid to stay with us. But I never heard back from them. Obviously, they didn't care about their grandchild."

"Oh, Shelly, that seems so mean. Maybe they didn't get the pictures," I said, wanting to make her feel better. "Where did you send them?"

"To their address in Karachi," Shelly said nonchalantly.

"Oh, I'm sorry they didn't respond to you," I said as I thought that Shelly had been through as much heartache as I had.

Shelly and I decided we wanted to visit Terezin Concentration Camp a short distance from Prague. It was a cold and windy day after the rain. The wind howled around the trees as we walked through the cemetery, making me think of the possibility of spirits hovering in the area. When I mentioned that to Shelly, she gave me a look as if to say 'don't be silly'.

Terezin was the largest Czech concentration camp during World War II. After walking through the camp, our guide took us to see the site of the Jewish ghetto, and the school which was now a museum.

I could see how it all affected Shelly as she tried to hold back the tears, just like I was trying to do. We rode back to Prague in relative silence due to our heavy hearts.

After that, we booked a day trip to Vienna, Austria. We had to leave early in the morning and didn't get back until almost midnight. It was a long ride on a tour bus, but we enjoyed seeing the sights. As we approached Vienna, our guide pointed to a large castle-like building on a hilltop overlooking the Danube. "That was the mental hospital for the royal family, the Habsburgs. There were so many members of their family who were mentally ill that they had their own mental hospital. It was because they kept marrying their first cousins."

"See!" I said as I elbowed Shelly in the ribs. She and I both laughed.

"Marrying first cousins doesn't cause mental illness in their offspring," Shelly said. "But if there's mental illness in the family, the chance of the children developing it is much greater. If you have two unrelated parents and one of them is mentally ill, your chance of developing it is, therefore, much less."

"That's good to know. I'm glad my parents weren't related." I leaned back and relaxed on the seat until we got to our first stop.

After a quick tour of the Schonbrunn Palace and its surrounding gardens, we got back on the bus and drove to an area of many restaurants where we had lunch. Soon it was time to get back on the bus, and then we headed back to Prague. Both Shelly and I were getting very sleepy on the return ride.

That night, after arriving back at our hotel, we fell into bed exhausted and planned to sleep in the next morning. When we awoke and looked out the window, we were very surprised. Much to Shelly's chagrin, there was a layer of snow on the ground, and it was still coming down.

"Well, I was right about the weather being bad this time of year," Shelly said, giving me an 'I told you so' look. "So far, we've had rain, cold winds and now snow. Let's stay in today, eat in the restaurant here and swim in the pool. Then we can relax and have a cup of tea after we swim," Shelly said as she slipped her feet into her sneakers. She was already dressed for winter weather in a heavy sweater and jeans.

After breakfast, we went back to our room and read, then went to the gift shop to check out their jewelry. In the afternoon, we swam in the Olympic size pool for a while before we got out, dressed and had tea in the lounging arca. Shelly was determined not to step outside in the snow, so we ate at the hotel again.

The following morning, it had cleared, but was still quite cold. However, we ventured out to nearby restaurants and even found a museum close by. Then it was time to pack up our belongings and head to the airport in the morning for our trip back to America.

We sat just inside the lobby waiting for our shuttle to take us to the airport. When it arrived, we went out with our luggage, and the driver held the door for us and put our suitcases in the back.

"I thoroughly enjoyed Prague," I said. "Thanks for coming with me." I fastened my seatbelt.

"I'm glad I came. It was magnificent to see all Prague had to offer." Shelly smiled and looked out the window as we passed out of the city.

Our flight home from Prague took us through Paris. We flew on Air France to Newark. My friend picked us up at the airport and told us they'd made plans for dinner that night. "Rose really wants to go out for Chinese food. I think it sounds good. Are you both feeling well enough, or are you too tired," my friend asked.

"I think it's a good idea," I said, glancing at Shelly who was nodding her head yes.

We drove to my place, put our luggage in the house and picked up Rose. We had a nice welcome home dinner with my friends. After we ate, we returned home and fell into bed. Shelly had to leave the next morning, and I had to go to work.

Our first trip together was so wonderful; we agreed we must continue to be travel companions.

CHAPTER TWENTY-THREE

After returning home, Shelly and I continued to talk on the phone about once a week. Sometimes, when one of us was super busy, we wouldn't have a chance to call, but we stayed in touch by sending a text to each other.

The same year, 2015, Shelly invited me to California to spend Christmas with her, Anita and their family. Since Jasim was in India again and both my girls had left New Jersey, I accepted the invitation. I was never used to celebrating Christmas in a big way, but I was looking forward to spending it with Shelly and Anita.

I shopped for days for her whole family and then spent hours wrapping the presents I would take with me. Laden down with gifts, I flew to San Diego where Shelly was waiting for me near the baggage claim area when I came down the escalator. Thankful that she was there waiting for me, I didn't have to worry about being left at the airport for a long time like I had been in New York when I couldn't find Rashid.

"I'm so glad you came to visit," Shelly said, taking my arm and leading me toward the baggage claim carousel. She helped me lift my suitcase to the floor.

As soon as we retrieved my luggage, we went out to Shelly's car and drove to Anita's house where she lived in a granny flat across the breezeway from the main house. "I wanted to be close to Anita and my grandkids, so they made a small apartment for me," Shelly said as she unlocked her door, and we walked inside.

Her apartment was small and cozy. She had a small decorated Christmas tree close to the entry, and it was surrounded by wrapped gifts. Shelly had cleared a portion of her closet, so I could hang some of my clothing. She had made room on a shelf for other items.

On Christmas Eve, we drove up a hill to her son-in-law, Sean's, brother's house for a family dinner and gift exchange. I was welcomed by everyone there. At least thirty people must have been in attendance. I received a present from Sean's mother, also. How sweet that was, I thought.

As we were leaving, Sean's brother pointed out to me that you could see the lights of San Diego from his house. I hoped to be able to go in the daylight for a better view, but never got the chance.

On Christmas morning, we were summoned to the main house for opening presents. Anita handed me a Christmas stocking along with everyone else. It was filled with lotions and other useful items. I was surprised by the gifts I received; a handmade white afghan from Anita and a picture book of our travel to Prague from Shelly.

It was enjoyable watching Anita's son, Brian with his two little boys, Angelo and Lorenzo, as they opened their many packages. There were squeals of delight as the wrapping on each gift was torn off.

After opening all the presents, we ate breakfast, and then Shelly and I went out sight-seeing in San Diego. It had been dark when my flight arrived in San Diego and other than the lights of the city, there wasn't much I could see as we flew into San Diego and landed. I had been surprised that the airport was so near the downtown high-rises; although, there are no skyscrapers due to the fact that the airport is so close to the buildings.

As we drove downtown and went past the airport, Shelly pointed out the naval base by the San Diego Bay, which is a natural deep-water harbor. Shelly drove us up a hill and then took me to the old light house and Cabrillo monument over-looking the San Diego bay.

"When I first came to San Diego, I used to drive here and sit out by the monument and meditate on my life. I was inspired looking at the bay and mountains in the distance. You can see the Pacific Ocean where it joins the bay, too. Over to the right you can see Tijuana on a clear day," Shelly said. "Unfortunately, it's too hazy to be visible today."

The following day, we drove to the border of Mexico and walked across into Tijuana. We hailed a cab and rode to downtown's main street, where we looked in shops and donned serapes and sombreros so we could have our pictures taken with them on. Later, we ate tacos for lunch at a small café.

"Are you ready to go back home, or do you want to see anything else here?" Shelly asked as we walked along the sidewalk, ignoring the many vendors hawking their wares.

"I'm ready to leave here. I've seen enough now," I said as we hailed a cab to take us to the border. Once there, we had to wait in line about two hours to get back to the US. Shelly was distraught.

"If I'd known we'd have to wait in line this long, I'd have driven across the border. This is too long to have to stand in line," she complained as she sat down on the curb.

"It's probably so long because of the holiday," I said as we began to inch along. Someone offered us a ride to the front of the line. Shelly paid him only to discover we were still far from the front. He'd taken us to a different line, but it was just as long.

Once we crossed the border, we got into Shelly's car, and she showed me some of the sights around the areas where she used to live. She told me stories about her marriage to a Mexican American and drove by the house they used to own.

"It looks different than when we lived here," she said. "We had a detached garage, but the new owners remodeled and built it into just another room connected to the rest of the house."

I was enjoying the tour, and at times I could picture how miserable Shelly had probably been over the years. "Do you think you would have been able to deal with Rashid's mental illness, if he'd stayed with you?" I asked as we drove back to her place.

"I honestly don't know," she said, turning to look me in the eyes. "He wasn't insane when we were together. As far as I know, he developed it right before he came to get a divorce. And then there were times he almost seemed normal, except for his delusional claims."

"Delusional claims?"

"Yes, he told me, when he was in the mental hospital in Brooklyn, that when the television was on, only pictures of Anita and me were on the screen. He also said they gave him newspapers with only our pictures, also. He said the government was out to get him as well."

"His doctor in Canada told me he was seeing the same thing when he was hospitalized there," I said, wondering why he'd see images of Shelly and Anita every time he was in the hospital.

"They must have had to restrain him by his wrists while he was hospitalized, because one of the first things he showed me was the marks on his wrists. He told me our government was out to kill him, so he was probably trying to escape."

"Yes, I imagine he must have been trying to escape," I said. "If he thought people were going to hurt him, he probably did try to get out of there."

"Yeah, probably so. I really felt sorry for him then. His parents had forced him to divorce me, and he must have had some guilt feelings over it," Shelly said as she pulled into their driveway. "My mother felt sorry for him for the rest of her life. She and my dad really liked Rashid."

The next morning after breakfast, we took off sight-seeing again. This time she took me to Old Town San Diego. We parked the car in a lot and then walked to the main street. After browsing some of the shops, she suggested we go to an Italian restaurant and have pizza. Although I'm not overly fond of pizza, I agreed to it.

When the waiter came to take our order, I asked if a certain pizza had pork in it. "No," he said, "it doesn't."

After he left, Shelly was smiling and asked, "Why is it you're so concerned about the possibility there may be pork in hamburger? You do know hamburger is beef, not ham." She laughed.

"I don't really eat much meat anyway, mostly chicken breast," I said as I picked up my glass of water and took a sip. "Besides, we are not allowed to eat pork in our religion."

"Yes, I know that," Shelly said. "However, Rashid never said a word about not being able to eat pork, and I'm sure he ate it at least a time or two. My mother would make bacon and eggs when we were there, and I never saw him turn down anything. He ate whatever was put before him."

"He was very strict about adhering to our religion when we were married," I said, remembering how he often prayed.

"He never adhered to anything in his religion when we were together. In fact, he went to church with me and didn't say anything about having to follow any of Islam's rules." Shelly took a drink of her soda and cut into her personal size pizza that had just been set in front of her. She looked pensive for a moment and then added,

"He and I even exchanged my Bible for his Quran when he left for England. So, I know he wasn't reading it much, or he wouldn't have thought to trade with me."

"I'm surprised," I said, wondering why he wasn't following our religion closely then.

"The first time I knew he'd started obeying Islam's rules was when I visited him in New York. He went into the bathroom and did a ritual wash and then got on his prayer rug and prayed. I was sort of surprised when he did that as I'd never seen him following Islam before," Shelly said and then took a big bite of her pizza and chewed slowly. "But in a lot of ways, he was like a different man then. Oh, he was still kind and loving, but some things were different. I guess it was his illness."

"You didn't know him," I said, meaning she didn't know the real man he was when I was with him during our marriage.

"You're right. I didn't really know the crazy man you were married to. I only knew the sane one I married," Shelly said as she laughed. "But then you didn't know him as a sane man." She gave me a smirk and then laughed even louder.

We stopped at a market that sold Indian spices and lentils. We bought a chicken, and with Shelly's help later that evening, I prepared a nice Pakistani dinner for the family. We carried it across the breezeway and ate with all Anita's family.

"Are you enjoying your visit to San Diego?" Anita asked as she served a chicken leg to one of her grandsons.

"Yes, very much," I said. "It's so beautiful here."

"The weather is one of the main attractions for me," Shelly said, looking over at me. "Its climate is mostly mild year-round. No snow, which I hate." She chuckled.

The next day, Shelly asked if I'd like to go to the zoo. The San Diego Zoo is world famous, and I thought I'd like to see what all it had to offer, but when we got there, the parking lot was completely full. "Would you like to go to Sea World instead?" Shelly asked.

"Yes. I'd like to see Sea World," I said as she drove us out of the parking area at the zoo. I looked over at the terrain as we passed through the area and saw that there were many canyons close to downtown San Diego.

"The park that we are passing is called Balboa Park, and it has many museums there. I wish we had time to tour some of them, but maybe the next time you come out we can go there," Shelly said as she pointed to a tall building close by.

When we arrived at Sea World, we parked the car and walked to the entrance. As soon as we entered, we stopped someone to take our picture. We didn't spend a lot of time there, but Shelly made sure we saw the penguins. They were so adorable in their habitat.

On Sunday morning, Shelly and I got dressed and went to her church. I was warmly welcomed by the people there. As soon as the service ended, Shelly drove us to an area called Point Loma where Steven's fiancée's bridal shower was being held. We met Anita and Natalie there.

After we ate a light lunch, Katie opened her many gifts. We were then served cake and shortly thereafter, we left to go shopping in Mission Valley.

Soon it was time for me to return to New Jersey. Anita, Sean and Shelly took me out to a Russian restaurant right before I needed to go to the airport. My luggage was packed and in Shelly's car, so she could drop me off after we ate.

"Thanks so much for the wonderful time I've had; the best Christmas celebration," I said as I got out of Shelly's car and she hugged me goodbye.

"I'm so glad you came to visit," Shelly said, getting back in her car.

After checking in, going through security and walking to my gate, I was told our flight to Newark, NJ was canceled due to a snow storm on the East Coast and we'd not be able to leave until morning. I called Shelly and told her.

"Shall I go pick you up and bring you here for the night? I can take you back to the airport in the morning," she said after I explained the situation.

"No. Our flight might leave too early, and I don't want to miss it. I need to be home in time for New Year's Eve. I have plans with Rose," I said.

"If you change your mind, let me know. I'll go get you. I hate to think of you spending the night in an airport."

I spent a miserable night in the San Diego airport, trying to doze until finally, we were told a flight was leaving very early that next morning. I decided right then I'd rather not travel during the winter months. I didn't want to have to go through sleeping in a chair at an airport ever again in my life.

When I finally arrived back in New Jersey, a friend picked me up at the airport and drove me home. I unpacked and got ready to go to the New Year's Eve party with my friend, Rose. She came to my house, and we walked to the senior center together. We entered the already bustling crowd and settled into chairs around a large table. With hats on and noise makers in our hands, we were ready for the New Year to begin and whatever new adventures it would have for us.

CHAPTER TWENTY-FOUR

I had reached retirement age, but didn't want to totally quit working. A part time position was open for me, and I decided to stay on teaching kindergarten for a while longer. It helped pay for my travels and gave me a feeling of still being useful to society.

When I wasn't working, I'd read or spend time with different friends. I had been blessed with many good friends in my life and enjoyed different activities with each of them.

Most of my many friends were American, except Rose, who was Italian, born in Italy. And I did have one friend, Patrina, from Croatia. My friend, Linda, was Japanese American and one of my friends was from India. I did meet a female Pakistani doctor, whom I became close to and began working in her office as a receptionist one evening a week.

I had a busy social life, since I was always invited to go to movies or dances and, sometimes, to parties or weddings. We had moved several years ago to a gated senior community and had joined many of the different clubs they hosted.

I joined the Emerald Club which was for Irish seniors. We were free to join any and all the different clubs, so we joined most of them. It kept us busy going to all the activities.

Hanna and her family had moved to Texas two years ago, and Saba had moved to Wisconsin to be with her boyfriend. I missed seeing them often and, on occasions, would have to travel to visit with them. I'd been to see both of them already and planned to visit at least once a year. I missed having my girls close to me in New Jersey.

Saba and Hanna had become close to their sister, Anita. They had both been to visit her and her family a couple of times already. Hanna and Jerry had even gone to Steven and Katie's wedding. It appeared my daughters had bonded with Anita, and it made Shelly and me very happy to know how well they got along. We kept blaming ourselves for not staying in touch, so they could have met many years before they did.

Jasim was in India taking care of business with the house he owned, and I was feeling the urge to travel again. I called Shelly and suggested we start planning another trip. "Where should we go this time?" I asked after our usual greetings.

"How about Ireland or Spain?" Shelly said.

"I've been to Spain, but I could go to Ireland with you," I said. "I'd really like to go to Greece and Turkey, too."

"Oh, I'd like to see those two countries," Shelly said with enthusiasm in her voice. "We could take a Mediterranean cruise that goes to both countries."

"That's a great idea," I said, thinking how wonderful a cruise would be.

"I'll check on it and see how much it would cost us," Shelly offered. "I'll let you know as soon as I find out."

Within a few days, I received a call from Shelly. "I found a Mediterranean cruise at a good price and the airfare to Venice, Italy is very good. Shall I book it for us?"

"Yes, and let me know how much I owe," I said with excitement in my voice.

"Tell me the dates you can go," she said.

"I'll look at my calendar and text the dates to you later tonight." I was so happy to think I'd finally be able to tour Venice, Italy as well as see Greece and Turkey.

Our plans were made for the following April, 2017 and we began the count-down until we could spend 10 days exploring new places. I received word that the cruise port in Turkey was closed, and we'd be stopping at another city in Croatia. Shelly and I were both disappointed that we couldn't see Turkey, but the cruise line said it was for the safety of both the crew and passengers. Terrorism had recently hit Turkey.

A short while later, Shelly called and asked if I'd like to go to the Dominican Republic with her for ten days the beginning of December, 2016. She was going with some friends and a few other people she didn't know. She was excited about spending time at a beach resort that time of year.

At first, I thought it might be nice, but then I changed my mind and decided not to go, since I'm not really a beach person. Later, when I saw her pictures from there on Facebook, I was glad for her that she had had a great time with her other friends.

Shortly before Thanksgiving, I called Shelly and told her that Jabeen's daughter, Niya, and her family lived in the San Diego area, and she should connect with her on Facebook. Shelly reported back to me that she and Niya had met for lunch and made plans to have both families meet. I was pleased that Anita was going to meet a first cousin, also.

In February, 2017, Shelly called to tell me she had another great grandchild. Steven's and Katie's daughter, Sofia, had been born. Shelly was so excited to have a new baby in the family.

Soon, I started counting the days off on the calendar until Shelly and I could travel together again. We seemed to have so much in common, that it was just incredible to believe. Once again, I thought about our similar likes and dislikes, and how much we enjoyed each other's company.

At school, I talked to my co-workers about my relationship with Shelly. I was always excited to tell them about our rapport. Some of my co-workers and friends were surprised that I could be close to Shelly, and they asked me why we enjoyed spending time together. I explained to them that, in just a short time, she'd become like a sister to me. We genuinely cared for one another.

I was talking to Shelly on the phone one day and told her my co-workers thought it strange that I could be friends with her, considering we had been rivals at one time.

Shelly laughed and said, "You and I should be in charge of world peace. We started out as enemies, and now we're best friends; more like sisters, really."

"You're right," I said. "The world leaders could learn a thing or two from us." I laughed loudly as I heard Shelly continue to laugh.

CHAPTER TWENTY-FIVE

In April, 2017, Shelly arrived at my house once again in preparation for our trip to Europe. Jasim was home this time, so he and I went to the airport in Newark to pick her up.

We had fixed dinner early and just needed to heat it up when we got home. We had fixed some of the Indian food we knew Shelly liked. It was the first time Jasim and Shelly had had the opportunity to really get acquainted, and the conversation flowed easily. It seemed they had respect for each other and that made me very happy.

The next morning, I went with Jasim and Shelly to Rose's house for breakfast and cappuccino before I had to report for work at nine o'clock. I would be off by one o'clock, and we'd have time for lunch before leaving for the airport.

Rose greeted us with a platter of fruit, along with eggs and toast. Then she served us her wonderful cappuccino. Shelly swore it was the best she'd ever had. "I never thought I liked cappuccino until I tasted yours, Rose," Shelly said as she picked up her cup and sipped.

"Thanks," Rose said as she beamed with pride. She fussed over us making sure we had enough to eat before she took her seat at the table.

When it was time to leave for school, I excused myself and drove to work. Jasim had planned to take Shelly to see the Hindu temple which was still being built, and then he was going to pick up Indian food for lunch, much to Shelly's delight. They were waiting for me to come home, so I could eat lunch with them. Rose had come to enjoy the lunch, also.

Immediately after we ate and put the left overs away, we got our luggage and headed out to the car. Jasim loaded our suitcases in the trunk and got in to start the engine. We arrived at the airport in plenty of time before our flight left for Amsterdam.

"Jasim is really a very nice man and so respectful," Shelly said once we got to our gate and found seats to sit on. "I'm glad I got to know him finally."

"Yes, he's a really nice man. He treats me so well now," I said as I looked out the window to see if our plane was already at the gate. It wasn't, but I saw a large plane on the other side of the terminal and wondered if it was our plane.

We were told there would be a delay, so Shelly and I walked around finding something to snack on and also to buy water. "I wish they would give us an update on our flight," Shelly said. "I hope this doesn't make us late in Amsterdam and cause us to miss our flight to Venice."

Finally, the large plane that was sitting at a gate across from us left that gate and came to ours. We were then told they'd had to let off international travelers there before it could come to our gate. We showed our boarding passes and passports and walked down to the plane. We found our seats and buckled in.

We had been delayed so long; we didn't get dinner served until quite late. Needless to say, neither of us got much sleep on the plane. When we arrived in Amsterdam, we were sleepy and tired, but still had to stand in a very long line for immigration.

Finally, an immigration employee came past the line and called for passengers who were booked on the flight to Venice. Shelly and I stepped out of line and followed him to a shorter line where our passports were checked and stamped.

At last we boarded our flight to Venice. We sat in our seats and closed our eyes. "I hope we'll be able to do some sight-seeing once we get there, but I'm really sleepy," Shelly said, opening one eye and peering at me.

"I hope we can," I said with a smile on my face. "I've always wanted to tour Venice."

"Of course, we still have a day in Venice once we come back from the cruise."

When we landed and got our luggage, we trudged outside to wait on our shuttle to the hotel. It was hot, and there was nowhere to sit and wait. When the van showed up, we climbed in, and it took us to the hotel. After checking in, we were told the hotel restaurant was closed, but we could take the van to a nearby restaurant for lunch.

A young man who introduced himself to us had just checked in also. "Do you mind if I ride to the restaurant with you and join you for lunch?"

"Sure, it's fine," I told him as I looked at Shelly. She was nodding her head yes.

We walked out to the van with him and got in. "I'm from the USA," he said when we left the van and walked toward the restaurant entrance. "I'm a pilot working for a wealthy businessman. We live in Switzerland. I just flew us here this morning." He held the door open for us.

"Do you come here often?" Shelly asked, glancing over her shoulder at him.

"Yes, my boss is Italian and we come here often, so he can take care of his business."

When we were seated, he advised us what was good to order off the menu. Shelly chose pizza, and he said, "Don't pick up a piece of pizza with your hands. The Italians consider it impolite."

"Really?" Shelly said with a shrug of her shoulders. When her pizza arrived, we were astonished at how large it was. I laughed to myself as I watched her cutting, or trying to cut through the crust. After eating less than half of it, she declared she was done and would take the rest back to our room. "I'll put it in the fridge in our room and then have it for dinner tonight."

By the time we got back to the hotel, we were both really sleepy.

"Let's take a nap now. After we wake up, maybe we can go out to sightsee," Shelly said as she sat down on the side of her bed.

"Yes, I'm sleepy, too," I said, kicking off my shoes and plopping down on my bed.

Shelly pulled the curtains closed and it made the room dark. Both of us snuggled into our beds and soon we were both sound asleep.

When we awoke, we freshened up and went to the restaurant to eat dinner. It was open then and we seated ourselves close to the door. "It's too late to go out sightseeing now," Shelly said. "Let's just plan to spend the day after our cruise touring the area, if that's okay with you."

"Yes, it's okay. It is too late to start out now," I said as I looked at the menu in front of me. As soon as we finished eating, we walked around the outside of our hotel and then went back to our room, showered and climbed back into bed.

The next morning, Shelly's left-over pizza went into the trash as we packed up our belongings and went to check out. We took a taxi to the port where our cruise ship was docked. After checking in, we got on board and went to have lunch. We checked out our room, which was an inside cabin, and then toured the ship while we waited for our luggage to be delivered to our room. Once it arrived, we unpacked and settled in for the week.

We were up on deck when we sailed away from port and past the islands around Venice. "Isn't it beautiful," I said as we stood by the railing looking out over the blue water. I took several pictures of the area.

"Yes, it is," Shelly said as she snapped a picture, too. "It's so wonderful to be out at sea." The look on her face was one of contentment and pleasure. She enjoyed seeing the beauty of nature, just like I do.

As soon as we ate dinner that evening, we went to the shore excursion desk and booked a couple of land tours at ports of call. The nightly show had started, and I went to see it. Shelly said she'd rather shower and then read for a while. When I returned, Shelly was already sleeping. I guess she was still tired from our journey the previous day. I got ready for bed and turned out the light. As I slipped into bed, I hoped I hadn't awakened Shelly.

"I think we've docked," I said as I rolled out of bed. Shelly was up and getting dressed. "I don't feel the ship moving now.

She looked at her watch and then said, "Yes, I think we're probably already in Croatia. Let's go up to the buffet and look out the window while we eat breakfast."

I grabbed my heavy black sweater and put it on as we walked out of our room. We took the elevator up to deck ten and entered the buffet area. There was so much food, it was unbelievable. We went through the line, selected our breakfast food and then found a seat close to a window. We looked out at the city of Dubrovnik and its surrounding area while we ate.

Waving his hand across the window expansively, a man seated next to us said, "Here's the 'Pearl of the Adriatic'. When Shelly and I both looked at him, he smiled and said, "That's Dubrovnik's nickname."

"Oh," Shelly and I both said in unison. We finished our coffee and headed to the theater to meet up with our tour group. After finding a seat, we waited for our tour to be called. Soon, we were summoned to leave the ship and board a bus.

The scenery was absolutely beautiful as we drove along the coastline up the hill overlooking the city. What a breath-taking view I thought as we looked down at the walls surrounding the old city right on the water. After taking pictures from above, we got back on the bus and drove to the old city entrance.

"Isn't it amazing to be in an old medieval town in Europe?" Shelly said as we walked down the slope and through the gates of the old city.

"It is truly amazing," I replied, looking at the high stone walls on both sides of us as we made our way toward Onofrio's Fountain which is connected to a seven and one-half mile aqueduct that has carried drinking water to the city for centuries.

Our guide pointed out to us that the streets were made of marble. They were shiny and clean. Shelly and I hung onto each other so we wouldn't slip and fall until we got used to the shiny surface that looked so slippery. As we walked along, we passed a Franciscan Monastery which is home to one of the oldest still functioning pharmacies in Europe. We wandered around the courtyard of the 14th century Gothic cloister and looked at the art hung on the walls.

Shelly and I sat at an outdoor café facing the City Bell Tower with churches surrounding the area and ordered drinks, a coke for Shelly and a juice for me.

As we were walking back toward our bus stop, the guide waved her hand in the direction of the building where some of the television series, Game of Thrones, is filmed. We gave it a cursory glance and walked on.

When we got back to our ship, we ate lunch and relaxed in the atria, watching people having their photos taken, and then we went out on deck and watched as we pulled away from dock and headed out into the Adriatic Sea again on our way to Montenegro.

The next morning, we awoke to a dreary day. We were docked in Kotor, Montenegro and looked out the window at the surrounding rocky mountains. They were beautiful, and the shrubs interspersed were colored forest green. It had rained overnight and there was a chill in the air.

Shelly and I had decided not to do a shore excursion there, but rather take the hop on, hop off bus to sight-see. As soon as we were cleared to leave the ship, we braved the cold and walked across a bridge to the corner of the street. It was directly across from the wall of the 'old town'. We waited there for the bus to arrive. Shelly was perturbed to see that the bus was open air; that is, it had no roof. We sat as close to the front as possible and still Shelly was freezing.

"I wish we hadn't taken this bus. I can't enjoy the scenery because I'm so cold," she complained as she shivered. A nice older man who was seated in the front row offered to let her sit there where the glass next to the door and also the windshield would help keep the wind from blowing directly on her.

We drove to the ruins of a Roman house to see the mosaic tile floors that had been unearthed during an excavation. After walking over all the different floors that had been in various rooms, we got back on the bus and headed back toward the dock.

Back at the port, Shelly and I decided to walk over to an outdoor café and have a cappuccino before going back on the boat. We sat at a table under an umbrella and sipped our drinks.

Although Montenegro was a beautiful place to see, we were happy to get back on the ship. We went to the buffet for lunch, and as soon as we ate, we ventured to our favorite spot outside the buffet. It was a small area on either side of the ship with a couch and two chairs. Two small tables sat between them. It was ideal for sitting and looking out the window while we talked. We had gone there on different occasions, sometimes taking our tea out to that spot to drink it and chat.

That day we talked about Rashid once again. We had gone to our little area by a window. "I don't think he loved me at all, now that you've told me a lot of things he'd said over the years. I was probably just someone to spend time with until he could escape back to his own country," Shelly said as she picked up her cup and sipped the tea. There was a look of sadness in her eyes.

"Oh, I don't think that's true at all," I said. I relayed to her what Rashid had told me about asking his father not to ruin his life, that he already had a wife and child.

"Really? I'm surprised. I thought he just obeyed his father and did what he was told. I do know he had conflicting feelings about it the last time I saw him in London when I took Anita to see him, or at least he seemed to have. One minute he would tell me he'd come back to us and the next, he'd say he couldn't go against his parents." Shelly took a drink of her tea and set the cup down on the table.

"I guess he would have conflicting feelings if he wanted to stay with you, but knew his father wouldn't let him," I said, feeling a little sadness for Shelly and Anita.

"He cried a lot during that time," Shelly said. "I think it was breaking his heart, also, or at least that's what I thought then. Later, when we were divorcing, he told my father and me that his father sent a couple of men to London to enforce his return to Pakistan." Shelly turned her head and glanced out the window at a small boat that was moving through the harbor.

"I don't believe his father sent anyone to force him into anything," I said, surprised that Rashid would say that. I didn't think it could be true.

Shelly looked like she was deep in concentration for a minute or two. Then she turned and looked at me again. "You do know that people with Schizophrenia sometimes see and hear people who aren't really there? Maybe that was the case with Rashid. If his father didn't really send anyone, maybe he saw them in his mind."

"I suppose that could have been what happened," I said, wondering if he saw and heard people who weren't there the whole time we were married.

When we finished our tea, we went out on the deck to walk around and see what was happening by the pool. Sometime they had music and dancing, and we would sit and watch.

Later that evening, we retired to our room after dinner to read and talk. We were about to move into another time zone and lose an hour, so we wanted to go to bed early.

Next on the agenda was Greece. We went to bed excited that soon we'd see a country we'd been enthusiastic about visiting. First stop was Olympia, where we saw the area where the first Olympic Games were held and then we sailed on to Athens. We had signed up for a coastline tour as well as sights of Athens, so we drove for a long distance and up a hill overlooking the Aegean Sea to the ruins of the temple of Poseidon. We learned that Poseidon was the Greek god of the sea and was equivalent to the Roman god, Neptune.

"I didn't know that," Shelly said as we sat down under the canopy covering the tables and chairs outdoors by a small restaurant. "I studied Roman mythology, but not Greek mythology."

It was then time to get back on the bus and head toward our next adventure. Back in Athens, we climbed the Acropolis and walked around the Parthenon. Shelly seemed to have a hard time climbing, and she had to rest several times going up the steep hill. "I'm going to have to go back to the gym when I get home. I'm really out of shape," she said, laughing. "I guess I've been eating too many noodles in my spicy stir-fry for lunch." I laughed with her.

When we got back to the ship, we discovered they were having Indian food at the buffet that night, so we hurried to get there to look it over and decide what we wanted. After eating a delicious meal, we went to our room. I got ready and went to the nightly show, while Shelly opted to stay and read before bed.

We had a whole day at sea, so we hung out on deck and took pictures. We took a few selfies, but were laughing so much we decided to ask the shore excursion employee if he'd take our picture out on deck. We had gotten numbers 1 and 2 from him and pasted them on our clothes; Shelly wore the 1 and I wore the 2. Then we had to explain to the shore excursion guy it meant she was wife number 1 and I was wife number 2. He howled with laughter along with us after we told him our joke. "I have to have a picture taken with you now," he said and then asked another passenger if he would take the picture.

Next stop was Split, Croatia, which had been in the province of Rome. In 305 A.D., Roman Emperor Diocletian built his palace and military garrison for his retirement. As we walked through the ruins of the palace and surrounding area, I was awestruck to be walking in a place that old. The palace was simply a complex of shops, bars and restaurants along the winding streets. We climbed up to the roof and looked down on the courtyard. There were three sphinxes over 3500 years old that had been brought to the city of Split from Egypt, exclusively for the emperor.

After touring the palace ruins, we stopped at the People's Square, an attractive piazza on the western side of the palace just outside the Iron Gate. It was next to the harbor. We ordered cappuccinos before heading back to our ship.

I don't remember how Rashid's name came up, but Shelly confessed to me, "I loved him very much. I was heartbroken when he told me his father ordered him to divorce me. I lost my appetite and couldn't eat for some time. All I did was cry. And I got really skinny."

I was overcome with sympathy for my friend, even though it had been a very long time ago. "I'm sorry you had to go through that," I said as we walked along by the harbor.

"It's okay. It was a really long time ago and I'm over it now, of course," Shelly said and then reached for my arm. "Let's go up on deck and get an ice cream."

The next morning, we arrived back in Venice. After we retrieved our luggage from the terminal and went through immigration, we went to a building which had lockers to store our luggage. When we entered, an older gentleman told us we could have our luggage sent directly to our hotel, so we wouldn't have to worry about getting it after we toured Venice. "Let's send them to the hotel," I said, and Shelly nodded her head in agreement.

We signed for the luggage and paid the fare. "Now we won't have to worry about getting them later," Shelly said as we put our receipts away and walked toward the taxi stand by the sea.

Free from encumbrances, we boarded the water taxi to downtown Venice. As soon as we got off, we checked our map and asked several people which way we should go to pick up our gondola ride. We started off and walked past St. Mark's Square, and then on to narrow lanes that abruptly stopped. We checked the map again and found that we were by the tour ticket office.

We sat down on a small ledge outside of a building. There was a small overhang that attracted several birds. While we were sitting there talking, one of the birds did his business all down the front of Shelly's purse and one of her pant legs. Out of nowhere, a man came and took wipes to start cleaning Shelly's purse and pants. She gave him a tip and he disappeared quickly.

"That means you're going to have good luck," I said, trying to make her feel better. She looked so distraught.

"If this is good luck, I'm not sure I want it," she said, and then laughed. "I don't see how that can bring good luck. It seems like bad luck to me. Sitting in the wrong place, at the wrong time."

After waiting for thirty minutes, we boarded the gondola with about four other people. One man in the back kept leaning over the side of the gondola. We all thought we were going to capsize, and an argument broke out between him and the man rowing. Shelly and I couldn't understand one word that was said, but we could tell that there were angry words spoken. Glad to be back on land, we headed back to the Grand Canal and took a water taxi to the airport where we could get a shuttle to our hotel. We were staying in the same hotel again, since it was close to the airport.

When we checked in, we were given a different room on the second floor. After putting our luggage in the room, we went downstairs to the restaurant and ate dinner. As soon as we were finished, we went to our room, showered and got into bed. We had to be up early the next morning for our flight home.

The next morning after breakfast, we packed up and left for the airport. We found our gate and settled on chairs to wait until we were called to board our plane. Once airborne, it was a little less than a two-hour flight to Paris, France where we changed planes. After going through immigration, we walked to where our plane was waiting. As soon as we boarded the plane, we checked what movies were playing and relaxed for thc long flight. Finally, we were on our way back to Newark, NJ.

Jasim was waiting for us in baggage claim and drove us to our house where he had already fixed dinner for us. Shelly loved his potato dish. "This has just the right amount of spice for me," she said as she took a second helping and another piece of naan. I could see Jasim beaming with pride at his culinary skill.

The next day around noon, Jasim loaded Shelly's suitcase in the trunk of his car. I had walked out with them and gave her a hug before she got in the passenger seat.

"I hope you don't mind that I'm not going to the airport with you," I said as I held the door open. "I need to relax before I have to return to work."

"I understand," Shelly said, smiling at me.

"I promise I'll go visit you in California again sometime during the year," I said as I shut her car door. I stood there and watched as Jasim pulled out of his parking space and drove away. I walked slowly back to our house and locked the door. Kicking my shoes off, I went to the living room and relaxed on the sofa for a while.

After a few hours, I realized I missed Shelly already. We had such fun together, laughing as we toured places and sharing many memories that we would have for years to come.

CHAPTER TWENTY-SIX

I had planned to retire the end of June, 2017, but my co-workers begged me to stay. I was at the age where I didn't want to deal with some of the hassles, so I madc a deal with them that I would continue to work part-time. Agreeing to work only for three hours a day, I gave up teaching kindergartners. I settled for working with four-year olds.

As much as Shelly and I love to travel, having extra income from part-time work would help defray the costs. When we were on the Mediterranean cruise, we decided we'd like to get a group together and go on a Baltic cruise. Jasim and Rose agreed it sounded like a good cruise and said they would like to go with us.

Two months after our cruise, I received another big surprise. My oldest daughter, Saba told me she and Norman were getting married on July 4th and asked Jasim and me to go to Wisconsin for their wedding. Rose had been invited also, since Saba considered her an aunt.

When we arrived on Sunday, Norman and Jerry picked us up at the airport and drove us the Edgewater Hotel where Saba and

Norman had made all the arrangements for the event. As soon as we checked in, we were greeted by Saba, Hanna and Anita. And I was delighted to see my granddaughters standing close to their mother. I was pleasantly surprised Anita had come for the wedding, also.

Once we settled in, we had lunch in the hotel restaurant. Over lunch, Norman said, "We're so glad you could come to our wedding."

"Oh, it's wonderful that you're getting married, and I'm glad to be here to witness it," I said as I looked from him to Saba. I was so excited, I could hardly think.

That evening, Saba and Norman had arranged to have Indian food catered in their apartment complex's recreation room. It was absolutely delicious and everyone seemed to enjoy it.

The next morning, I couldn't wait to call Shelly and tell her about the wedding that was to take place. Saba had admitted to me a couple of weeks earlier that it was her wedding I'd been invited to and not just a reunion. However, I'd been sworn to secrecy. She didn't want anyone else to know until after the fact.

"I know," Shelly said after I told her.

"You knew?"

"Yes, but not until Friday night. It was only a couple of days ago, and I'm sure Anita only told me because I asked her if she had to work Monday," Shelly said. "I told her I didn't think you knew because you hadn't said anything about it."

"I guess Saba wanted to surprise me, but she ended up telling me a couple of weeks ago," I said as I glanced over at everyone standing around waiting for me to get off the phone. "Anyway, I've very happy."

Saba had arranged for a spa day Monday morning. We had options of what we wanted. Rose and I chose to have our hair styled, Hanna chose to have a massage and Anita chose to have a manicure. After we were finished at the spa, we spent time in a beautiful park by the lake just outside the hotel.

Mexican food was chosen for lunch that day with Cajun food served for dinner. I was surprised that Saba and Norman had chosen such an array of ethnic foods for all their guests.

Tuesday morning, I was dressed in navy blue slacks and a matching printed silk blouse for the wedding. Saba was dressed in a short white lacy dress with a royal blue sash around the waist. Her hair was pulled back in a bun at the back of her neck with black decorative clips across the top of her hair. She looked so beautiful that morning.

We were taken to the aviation center for breakfast and the following wedding ceremony. On July 4th, 2017, Saba and Norman were married inside an airplane. Novel idea, they said. I'd hoped and prayed for several years that they would marry, and now it was coming true, I thought as I watched them saying their vows to each other as the plane flew over Madison, Wisconsin.

The vows were untraditional, but just what they had wanted. I was impressed with the vows when I heard them. Based on a Dr. Seuss book, Saba declared 'I'd marry you in a boat', and Norman responded 'I'd marry you with a goat'; then Saba said, 'I'd marry you in the rain' and Norman declared, 'I'd marry you on the plane'.

Only parents, siblings and their families were invited, so there were only about seventeen people present. The plane only had about ten seats and, therefore, had to make two trips to accommodate everyone. So, Saba and Norman had to say their vows to each other twice. Champagne was passed around to everyone on the plane, and we all toasted the bride and groom, wishing them well in their married life.

Then afterwards, there was a small reception dinner at the Edgewater Hotel restaurant. Saba had changed into a turquoise floor length gown for the dinner. Since American food was served, I ordered salmon and it was delicious.

That night, as I got ready for bed, I thought it had been the perfect wedding for my Saba. She deserved happiness and I was so glad she'd found it with Norman.

Jasim, Rose and I flew back to New Jersey the following day. I sat on the plane thinking that I was the happiest mother in the world, because both of my daughters were married now. I didn't need to worry about them now, I thought, since they have husbands to take care of them. And as a bonus, I'd been able to spend time with my two lovely granddaughters, also. They are always a delight in my life.

I had thought my summer would be relaxing, however, I was called to substitute teach for several weeks over the summer. A couple of teachers had resigned and the school was desperate for help. How could I refuse them? I thought as I got up and readied myself for work. I had to admit that I was happy when I was working, because it gave me a useful purpose in society.

I had talked to Shelly about the possibility of going to California again.

"Why don't you come in August?" Shelly asked as we were talking about the possibilities. "It won't be cold and snowy for your travel then."

"I think I might like to go there in November. I have several plans already for this summer," I said.

"Okay, plan on coming then. I can take you to see Niya, and since she lives close to the San Diego Safari Park, maybe we can go there the same day," Shelly said. "Just let me know when you finalize your plans."

"I will," I said right before we disconnected our call. I began making plans to go to California in November. Hoping to see Niya while I was there, I decided to call and ask Jabeen to visit at the same time. We hadn't seen each other in a very long time and it would be nice to have a reunion with her and her family. And Niya and I could introduce Jabeen to her niece, Anita and, of course, Shelly. I would have to wait and see if she would be able to go during that time.

A few weeks later, I received a text from Shelly asking if I'd like to go to Israel with her. Her church was planning a trip to the Holy Land and she was excited about the prospect of going there again. I have always wanted to visit Israel and I sent her back a text saying 'yes'. I now had another potentially wonderful trip to look forward to with Shelly.

The middle of August our Emerald Club hosted a one-day fun cruise. Jasim, Rose and I signed up for it. It was a warm day and pleasant out on the water. The ship cruised along the Raritan River toward Perth Amboy which is located in the northern area informally referred to as the Bayshore. As we floated past the historic waterfront, which is characterized by a redbrick promenade, I noticed the many stately Victorian homes on hills overlooking the bay.

The dinner selections were chicken, beef or pasta with different types of salads. I had a small piece of chicken, but ate mostly salad. As soon as dinner was over, the music started and we danced for the remainder of the cruise.

When the boat pulled into the dock, we walked off feeling quite exhausted. As soon as we got home, I went straight to bed and fell asleep.

The next morning, I cleaned the house and then spent some time pruning and watering my houseplants. A couple of them were beginning to look neglected, but with some tender care they looked like new plants.

After lunch, I sat down to read a book and ended up taking a short nap on the sofa. Surprised when I awoke, I realized I hadn't been resting as much as I should.

I was looking forward to a relaxing evening since Jasim had gone out to see some friends. I brewed a cup of tea and carried it into the living room. Turning on the television, I sat down on the sofa and put my feet up. As I sipped my tea, I reflected back over the last several years of my life. I thought about how thankful I am for all my family and friends. I was also thankful for the fact that Shelly had told me she prayed for me every day. It made me feel warm inside to think she would pray fervently for me.

A smile crossed my lips as I contemplated the possibility of spending more time with my many friends and having many more years of travel with Shelly.

As I sat there thinking about my life, I realized that I needed to forgive those who had deceived me when I agreed to marry Rashid. Yes, I was definitely the 'deceived wife', but out of it came the opportunity to meet my best friend, Shelly, with whom I have so much commonality. When I have a problem, it's her I call. If I need advice, I'll ask Shelly. I know in my heart she'll be honest with me, and I love her for that. And if God had given me a chance to choose someone for a sister, I would've chosen Shelly.

In Kotor, Montenegro
Shelly on the left and Ambreen on the right

CPSIA information can be obtained
at www.ICGtesting.com
Printed in the USA
FSOW03n0717080118
43163FS